If I had the wings of a sparrow,
If I had the arse of a crow,
I'd fly over Tottenham tomorrow,
And shit on the bastards below.
                              Old Song

Putting the Boot In

By Dan Kavanagh

Duffy
Fiddle City
Putting the Boot In
Going to the Dogs

Putting the Boot In

DAN KAVANAGH

An Orion hardback

First published in Great Britain in 1985 by Jonathan Cape Ltd
This edition published in 2014 by Orion Books,
an imprint of The Orion Publishing Group Ltd
Orion House, 5 Upper Saint Martin's Lane
London WC2H 9EA

An Hachette UK Company

1 3 5 7 9 10 8 6 4 2

A CIP catalogue record for this book
is available from the British Library.

ISBN (Hardback) 978 1 4091 5023 7
ISBN (Ebook) 978 1 4091 5025 1

Typeset by Deltatype Ltd, Birkenhead, Merseyside

Printed in Great Britain by CPI Group (UK) Ltd,
Croydon CRO 4YY

The Orion Publishing Group's policy is to use papers that are natural,
renewable and recyclable products and made from wood grown in sustainable
forests. The logging and manufacturing processes are expected to
conform to the environmental regulations of the country of origin.

www.orionbooks.co.uk

To Antonia and Martin

Warm-up

There are too many ways of breaking a footballer's leg. Too many, that is, from the footballer's point of view. Others may find the freedom of choice encouraging.

Duffy patrolled the edge of his penalty area and wondered what had happened to Danny Matson. That was where it had started. Danny Matson in the underground car park. The first sign of the whole business going public. And after it had gone public, and really threatened to become a bit serious, there had been more things to worry about than poor little washed-up Third Division Danny. Who remembers yesterday's footballers? Who remembers even the famous ones – the ones with the hacienda-style house, the Merc and the wife that's a genuine blonde, the ones who get to partner fat comedians on the TV golf? They slip the mind as soon as they stop playing. Pampered swaggerers, they strut the floodlit pitch for the last time, salute the fans, and disappear down the tunnel. Suddenly, they find it's colder there, and they don't feel so tall, and no one applauds; there's a faint smell of piss and Ajax, a forty-watt bulb overhead, and a concrete floor underneath. No grass any more: if you fall, this time it will really hurt. And that tunnel is the rest of your life. So if it feels like this to the players at the top, what chance was there for the Danny Matsons?

Time to stop worrying; or to start worrying about

something different. That speedy little ginge had got the ball again. Duffy retreated towards his goal. Close him down, for Christ's sake close him down. Bell was too slow, as usual, but Maggot got near enough to threaten a little GBH, so the ginge whipped the ball out to the left instead. Duffy checked his angles, got up on his toes, banged his gloves together and started inching out for when the winger beat the right back. He would beat the back, of course: he'd done him three times already, no trouble. Once going inside, once outside, once nutmegging him in a show of public contempt. Which would he go for this time?

He went for simple pace – the cruellest method there is. Show the full back every inch of the ball, give him a couple of yards, then just hare past him as if to say, Give it up, this game, don't bother, you're too fat, you're too slow, you're not smart enough. And that left it up to Duffy. Come out fast, narrow the angle, cut down the winger's options, make him pick one way or the other, don't go down too soon, but when you do go down, really spread yourself. Duffy was muttering the coaching manual to himself for company; there wasn't much other help around. The winger was closing fast. *Now*, thought Duffy, and started to spread himself. Just as he did so, the winger gave a little jink to the right, and took off at speed to the left. He beat Duffy, who couldn't lay a finger on him, legal or illegal; but in doing so ran himself out of space. Too close to the line, and with a red-faced defender thundering back, the winger tried a finely angled cross-shot which missed even the side-netting. He spat angrily and interrogated the turf, as if the ball had bobbled unexpectedly at the last minute. Duffy got up calmly, trying to look as if he had masterminded the whole thing. Honour seemed even, except that Duffy knew there would be a next time, quite soon, and that this fellow had more tricks than the Magic Circle.

Duffy was a worrier. They say goalkeepers tend to be worriers. Some start off like that, and choose to play in goal because it fits their temperament. Others start off calm, capable fellows and then get frazzled up by their own leaky back four, or by a sudden loss of form when their handling goes and they sweat at the thought of a high cross, or by some psychotic striker with Aberdeen Angus thighs who doesn't seem to know whether it's the keeper or the ball that he's meant to be putting into the net. Further up the park and you can hide; you can even blame others. But a goalkeeper is exposed. Everything he does wrong is vital. Ten men can win you the game and one berk can lose you it; that's what they say. You can get your own back a bit by shouting at the other ten: keepers are allowed to shout, and can sometimes shift the blame after a goal by picking out the least forceful member of the defence and giving him a rollocking. But mostly you're on your own, shuttling between boredom and fear.

Duffy had been a worrier long before he started playing for the Western Sunday Reliables. He'd been a worrier since – oh, he couldn't remember. He worried about that too: was his memory going? When other keepers went about their business, they worried about playing badly, and losing, and letting the side down, and getting kicked, and facing penalties, and getting called a wally. Duffy worried about all this too, and then some; he even worried about why he'd become a goalkeeper in the first place. Perhaps he wasn't really a worrier; perhaps he was a fully-fledged neurotic.

One of the reasons he liked goalkeeping – and one of

the reasons he worried – was that he liked things neat. He liked the neat box of the penalty area; he liked the way it marked out his territory, his manor. Everything that happens inside this box is your responsibility, Duffy; he felt like some young copper being given his first beat. He also liked the way everything in his manor had corners: the penalty area, the goal area, the woodwork; even the netting was made in squares. He liked these right-angles: they reassured him. The only thing on his patch that didn't have corners was the penalty spot. A great big round chalky mess, as if some bloody enormous pigeon up above had decided to unload right into the middle of Duffy's manor: *splat*. Somebody ought to clear that mess up, Duffy thought. It bothers me. He didn't like the penalty spot. For a start, it was much too near the goal.

He found himself looking down at his legs, at the white bits, the bits that were getting cold. A late March wind was blowing across the recreation ground. He wasn't looking for goose-pimples, though; he was looking for little brown blotches. Still doing so, after all these months. He was probably safe now; probably. But at the time, when that whole business was going on, it had been just another thing to worry about. Actually, to get shit-scared about. There were a lot of very frightened people down at the bars and clubs then, and Duffy had been no exception. There were days when someone had only to put a hand on his arm for Duffy to send his jacket to the cleaners. And the funny part of it – yes, it was funny, he decided, looking back – was the thing about Carol. The thing with Carol. Very odd. Duffy smiled.

Christ, that ginge again. Anyone would have thought the chief scouts of Juventus, Benfica and Manchester United lay concealed among the mute crowd of eight spectators that the game had attracted. Close him down, close him down, Duffy found himself yelling, even though the ginge was still in his own half. Bell had a go, with the usual lack of success, Maggot was caught too wide, everyone else backed off or stuck tight to the man they were meant to be marking, and suddenly the ginge was free and heading straight towards Duffy's manor. He came out fast. Where was his defence? Where was his fucking defence? Duffy had only one idea – get out there, outside the area, and bring the ginge down.

Perhaps the Benfica scout really was present. Duffy came roaring out, and had almost reached the edge of his box when he noticed something odd. The ginge had stopped running towards him. In fact he'd stopped running altogether. He'd put his foot on the ball. Before Duffy could cover another yard the freckly little fellow had flipped the ball up a couple of feet and volleyed it dippingly over the oncoming keeper; he was already turning away, index finger raised in modest triumph, by the time the ball hit the back of the net. One–nil.

Christ, thought Duffy. And they're only meant to be a pub team. Where had *he* sprung from? Had they brought in some cowboy specially? That didn't seem likely: everyone knew you didn't need cowboys against the Western Sunday Reliables. Perhaps he was some minor-leaguer coming back after injury and getting in a bit of extra match practice. Or perhaps he was just a chap who drank at the pub and happened to be a class above everyone else on the pitch. Somebody would certainly have to give *him* a whack pretty soon, or he'd be getting above himself.

The Reliables didn't even go through the motions of blaming one another. One or two nodded at the ginge as if to say 'Good goal'. Duffy wondered if he would have had any chance of touching the shot if he'd been taller; or if he'd jumped. The only trouble was, it wasn't so simple to jump when running full tilt; and if you did so, you'd probably signal it so obviously that the bastard would just toe-poke the ball along the ground underneath you instead, and then you'd really look a wally. This was one of the problems with goalkeeping. You needed to be several different sizes all at the same time. If you were tall, you could pick out high crosses all afternoon but got beaten by low volleys. If you were small, your ground work might be terrific but you often made the net seem invitingly large to opposing forwards. If you were chunky, there was a lot of you to spread in front of someone with the ball, but you might not be so nimble about the box. And if you were slim, you might move fast, but you might also find yourself on the end of a lot of agg when they brought up the big men for the corners. Duffy was medium-sized – just tall enough for the copper he'd once been years ago – and stocky. This seemed to him to be the worst of all worlds. It worried him.

One–nil. There goes my clean sheet, thought Duffy. He liked that phrase: 'keeping a clean sheet'. It made you understand the way goalkeeping was all about neatness, tidiness. He sometimes imagined conversations which went like this: 'How did you get on yesterday, Duffy?' 'Oh, clean sheet again.' He had to imagine these conversations because they very rarely took place. Not many people asked him about his football; and when they did he wasn't very often in a position to give the response he dreamed of. Clean sheet. It was a funny expression. He gave a small smile. The only time he'd kept a succession of clean sheets had been when he was searching his legs for brown blotches and taking his temperature every

8

other day; the time when the Alligator and all the other clubs were running scared.

The Reliables weren't the greatest outfit Duffy had ever played for. Some of them were a bit fat, a bit bald, a bit heavy in the leg; one or two of them were distinctly old. But they were keen; they turned up. It's all very well having a teamful of ball-playing wizards, but if only nine of them show up, and one of those nine happens to run into a skilfully placed elbow early on, then you're in trouble. Duffy had kept goal for a few Sunday teams like this. The trouble with Sunday is that it follows Saturday, and as likely as not the creative midfield dynamo has been creatively on the piss until all hours the previous night, while the hunky ballwinner is gazing round some strange bedroom for the first time and realising that he has six and a half minutes to get across London *and* he hasn't got his kit with him. Duffy had had enough of such teams; for a start, they tended to leave their keeper a little short of protection. Whereas with the Reliables, you could always count on there being four players in the back four. When the team had been founded, all of three years ago, they'd called themselves the Western Sunday Casuals. It sounded pretty smart, and even hinted that they were some rather posh outfit who'd been going since the days when everyone wore pyjama tops and shorts down to their calves; but it didn't really suit, and after a few months the Casuals had quietly become the Reliables.

One–nil with ten minutes to half-time. A couple more scares for Duffy, but otherwise not too bad. They'd really have to sit on the ginge, though; maybe kick that winger about a bit too. And perhaps last night's beer might catch up on the pub side in the second half. Just keep the concentration going and don't try anything clever in the last couple of minutes. Go two down and they'd be sunk. Lost. Lost without trace. Like ... like Danny Matson. Where was Danny Matson now?

First Half

There are too many ways of breaking a footballer's leg. If you want to make quite sure, of course, you can simply drop a few hundred in the right direction and the delivery man will come round with a junior sledgehammer in his pocket. That's a bit noisy, of course, but then it's surprising how many people don't mind being a bit noisy. If you want to be quieter, you might look up the right fixture, look up the right player on the other side – someone with good strong legs himself, for a start – and send a runner round to suggest a way of earning a little nest-egg. All for one awkward, mistimed tackle, a bit of over-the-top for a fifty-fifty ball, probably wouldn't even get a yellow card. However, there are even quieter ways.

Danny Matson was a bit pissed; even he would have admitted that. But the men who stopped him from taking his car out of the underground park that night weren't primarily concerned with cutting down the number of drunken drivers on the roads. Later, Danny couldn't even be sure how many of them there had been. 'How many would you estimate?' the detective-sergeant had asked him. 'Too bloody many,' was all Danny could reply. It had puzzled the detective-sergeant. Danny had only been carrying about thirty quid: hardly enough for a couple of lagers each nowadays.

Danny had been feeling pretty good that Saturday.

His twelfth first-team game on the trot. He'd fitted in; he'd done the business; and he'd laid on the pass for big Brendan to knock in the equaliser. He'd done some fancier things in the other games – five goals in eleven matches can't be bad for a midfielder, and especially when the team's struggling – but this time he'd been pleased with his all-round game. The lads had been pleased. The Boss had been pleased. They'd got a result. One–one against Barnsley wasn't rubbish in anyone's language. 'I see light at the end of the tunnel, lads,' the Boss said afterwards. The Boss always had this posh way of talking.

And the nice thing about getting a result, for a change, was that it made the rest of Saturday more lively. Sure, they'd get drunk regardless; but getting drunk to celebrate one–one against Barnsley was so much better than getting drunk to forget about getting thrashed. It also meant that you could look the bouncer in the eye when you turned up at The Knight Spot.

That was another nice thing about making the first team: they gave you free entry at The Knight Spot. Free entry; the first drink on the house; and at some point Vince would wander over and have a chat about the game. The time Danny had tucked away that header at the far post and given Athletic their first win in eight outings, Vince had come along with the ice bucket and the champagne. Personally. That was one reason people liked The Knight Spot: Vince wasn't above doing things himself.

So they'd had a bit of a knees-up that Saturday. A few of the lads were there and more than the odd Bacardi got drunk. Danny was even asked to dance by a girl called Denise, a bouncy, dark girl with more than a fair handout of flesh: most of it showing, and some of it pressed against

Danny. Tasty. I wonder what two–one against Barnsley would have earned me, Danny reflected. He thought Denise looked more than all right under the strobe lights.

When Monica turned up – Monica that he'd dated a couple of times recently – Denise chased her off. Not pushy; just firm. A few more Bacardis got themselves drunk, and when it was time to go Denise seemed to be with him. As far as the door, anyway.

'You fetch the car round, love, there's an angel,' she whispered, shivering a little and parting from his arm, it seemed, with the greatest reluctance.

Whoops, he thought, steady now, as he had a little trouble with his feet. They were getting uppity; didn't seem at all keen on walking him to the car park. Perhaps they knew something he didn't.

He got to the first basement level and set off in an approximately straight line towards his old Cortina. He hoped Denise wouldn't be too disappointed. Just waiting delivery on the new Capri, he thought he might mention. There were lots of things wrong with the Cortina. Like the way its keys kept playing hide-and-seek in your pockets. Ah, there they were. Now, mind that puddle. Funny how they never worked out the drainage in these car parks. There were always great lakes of oily water around even when it hadn't been raining for days. Now, which way up did the key go?

He thought they hit him on the head first, but later he couldn't be sure. They certainly knocked him down and gave him a bit of a kicking and rolled him in the water and messed his suit and nicked his wallet and tore off his watch. He was drunk enough to find it a matter of curiosity why they were doing all this to him, and why they were being so rough when they already had his wallet.

Why they were still holding him down, one of them sort of pushing his face into the oily water, and another one holding him by the leg. Perhaps he was trying to kick them; he wasn't sure. There was no noise except for some scuffling and panting, and by the time Danny thought to let out a bit of a shout they had given him good reason to do so. Maybe he had been kicking or something, because all of a sudden he felt this tremendous thump on the back of his ankle, just down near the heel. Then another, sharper this time, and another, and another, and suddenly more pain than he'd had from any injury in his career so far, even that shoulder he'd once put out at Scunthorpe. He screamed, and when he stopped screaming the men had gone, and his suit was messed, and his Rolex was stolen, and Denise had given up and gone home, and his career was wrecked.

Jimmy Lister was in his first season as manager of Athletic, and quite possibly his last as well. Fourth from bottom of the Third Division with ten matches to go. Every manager in the land knew what that meant. They wouldn't sack you before the end of the season because anything, they reckoned, was better than nothing as a manager; and no new fellow would take on the job at that stage. So you had the next ten games. If the team was relegated, you were slung out – no question. On the other hand, if you saved the team from relegation, that didn't make you a hero. Thanks but no thanks. Well done, Jim lad, good effort over the last six weeks, but I think we'll be making other arrangements at the start of next season. No hard feelings?

There were a lot of jokes about Jimmy having no hair left after a year in charge of Athletic; but the fact was, he didn't have much when he joined. He'd lost most of it by the time he'd finished as a player, so the stress that was getting to him now was probably going somewhere else. Ulcers, he expected.

He'd had a good run, on the whole, had Jimmy Lister. Started off as a wing-half in the days when such things still existed. Not quite the best, but pretty classy all the same. Three England B caps; a dozen years in the First Division, then three in the Second; and he'd come out of it all with a good reputation. Bit of a thinker, they said of Jimmy; bit of a card, too. He curled a nice cross-ball into the box, did Jimmy. A good reader of the game, they said; never played the obvious ball; always ghosting in from deep positions without being picked up. They said a lot of other junk about Jimmy Lister's game, and he was crafty enough never to deny it. Go bald and they immediately think you must be brainy; well, if that's what they wanted.

He made the jump into management early, and avoided that depressing slide through the divisions towards some Mickey Mouse team in the Toytown League. Two years as assistant, then three in charge of a Second Division club in the West Midlands. Sixth in the table when he took over; nineteenth when he left. Not brilliant. Not disastrous, either; not really. And there'd been the usual frustrations: not enough money to buy new players, because not enough people through the turnstiles; not enough people through the turnstiles because no exciting new players for them to come and see. Too many sag-bellied senior citizens nearing the end of their careers; a number of new lads coming along, but not coming along all that quickly. One really good find, quick lad, clever as a monkey, and the Board sells him to pay off the overdraft. One reason we've got an overdraft, he told the Board, is that we're selling lads like this one before they've had a chance to pull in the crowds. We admire your loyalty to your players, Jimmy, they told him; but we've got a loyalty to someone with a big stick called the bank. You'd rather have a bank manager than a football manager, he'd said. Don't get cheeky with us, Jim lad, or we'll have to let you go.

Just before the end of his third season somebody had tipped off the local paper about him and the physio's wife. All that free booze poured down the sports page and look what they do to you when you're on the ropes. The job went; Mrs Lister thought she'd call it a day too; it was a bad time. He had a year away from the game: did a little schools' coaching, just to keep his eye in; wondered about going overseas; and for a year he didn't buy himself a new shirt. When the call came from Melvyn Prosser he was finding it easy to get depressed. He didn't know who to thank, so he thanked Melvyn Prosser. Whoever he might be.

Athletic's trouble had always been that they were one of the least glamorous teams in London. Cup semi-finalists in the middle thirties, decent run one year in the League Cup, a few bits of yellowing silverware in the boardroom; but year in, year out, a team of huffers and puffers who never looked like blowing anyone's house down. The Board's answer had been Melvyn Prosser (or at least Melvyn Prosser's chequebook); and the new chairman's answer had been Jimmy Lister.

Jimmy had decided to play this one a bit more high profile. Image isn't everything, but it's not nothing. You buy a foreign player, for instance: he isn't necessarily better than someone you could have picked up for less money in Scotland, but a Dashing Dane or a Swanky Slav makes good copy in the local paper, and brings a few more in through the turnstiles, if only out of curiosity. It was the same with a manager. It couldn't do any harm to let them know there was a bit of a character loose among them, could it? And this time, he promised himself he'd keep his hands off the physio's wife, however tasty she might turn out to be.

He dressed himself carefully: the blue double-breasted blazer, striped shirt, scarlet tie, grey slacks, white shoes. A sort of bald Robert Redford, he thought. And always the white shoes, even in the rain. He'd thought of a fedora, but that had been done before; besides, the bald head was an item in itself. And the white shoes were a good touch. He did well by the press; he was always available; he opened a couple of shops in the first week after taking over; and he was pictured in the local paper with Miss West London sitting on his lap. He rang up the Playboy Club and asked for the loan of eleven Bunnies to do a photocall with the first team. He was given to understand that Athletic were not considered glamorous enough to merit the loan of Bunnies. But that's why I want them, he answered, to make us glamorous.

When he told Melvyn Prosser of this snub, the chairman said, 'I expect we could get the Dagenham Girl Pipers.'

Melvyn and Jimmy understood one another. Instead of the Bunnies, they hired a biplane to fly over the ground at half-time with a big banner attached to its tail reading COME ON YOU BLUES. The Blues were two–nil down at the time, and some of the crowd suggested that the plane's petrol money should have been kept in the piggy bank and put towards a new player. So the next week six girls dressed in Athletic strip came out before the game and each kicked a free football into the crowd 'with thanks from Melvyn Prosser', as the public address announced. Two of them were thrown back.

Athletic started the season well, with three home wins on the trot; they got through the first two rounds of the Cup without any trouble, but had the misfortune to land a tough set of Second Division doggers in the next round. Away from home; robbed in the last minute by an offside goal.

'Pity about that, Jimmy,' said Melvyn. 'Nice little Cup run would have done us a world of good.'

'Still, it leaves us free to concentrate on promotion,' said Jimmy. The remark was a little speculative, given that Athletic were then fourteenth in the table.

'You didn't say relegation, did you, James?' Melvyn inquired.

'No, no.'

'I'm glad to hear it. For your sake as well.'

The only trouble with concentrating on promotion was that there were many other sides in the Division with better powers of concentration. The bad weather came; they redesigned the players' strip, and got a decent news story out of it; they tried bingo in the official programme; but the team continued to slide. In early February Melvyn called Jimmy into his office. He had a way of standing, did Melvyn; sort of not quite looking at you, as if you weren't really central to his scheme of things, as if he was really addressing some misty figure a few yards behind you who might well turn out to be your successor. It unnerved Jimmy a bit.

'Jimmy, you know the trouble with this team I've bought?'

'I'm always listening.'

'It's a dog. That's what's wrong with it. A bow-wow.'

'So what do we do about it?'

'What *we* do about it, James, is that *I* tell *you* what to do about it. If it's a dog, then there's only one thing to be done.'

'Chief?'

'You must teach it new tricks.'

'Yes, chief.'

It was time to take risks. He pensioned off a couple of senior citizens whose legs were falling behind their brains, introduced Danny Matson and another scrapping youngster, pushed big Brendan Domingo further forward, demanded more fight, sympathised with players shown the yellow card, and indicated more openly than before which of the opposing players he expected to be shut down at all costs. His job was on the line, and this was the bottom of the Third Division. Keep it tight, take no prisoners, and push the big men forward whenever you get a corner. Back to basics.

None of this gave much pleasure to the former England B wing-half, who could still curl a ball in more accurately than those he managed; and it gave him mixed feelings when the change of tactics worked. They picked up a few points, climbed a couple of places, but still weren't out of the wood. Little Danny Matson had worked, though: come on fast, seemed to have struck up a real understanding with big Brendan. The coloured fellow was gaining a lot of confidence from having Danny always prompting him; he'd pointed this out to Melvyn, and Melvyn had agreed. He'd pointed it out because even Melvyn could see most of the other changes Jimmy had made – like the fact that his team were fouling a lot more vigorously than they used to – but you had to have a bit of a smell for the game to see how Danny and Brendan were knitting together.

What an idiot the boy had been. Jimmy had seen it before with lively little players like him. Full of fire on the pitch, can't believe it isn't the same off it. Put a win bonus under their belts and a few Bacardis in their bellies – or even the thrill of a draw plus a half of lager – and they start picking fights. The worst ruptured Achilles tendon he'd seen in twenty years of professional football. At least six months out of the game; possibly more. What they said about the Achilles tendon was always true in Jimmy's experience: however well it mends, you always lose a yard or two of pace afterwards. And Jimmy had seen enough football to know that Danny's game was all about pace.

Jimmy knew something else as well: that when the day came for him to be sacked, Melvyn would be very nice to him, and would call him James.

Duffy had had the flat in Goldsmith Avenue, Acton, for three years now. It looked as if he had moved in two days ago and the rest of his stuff hadn't arrived yet. But there wasn't any 'rest of his stuff', this was it: bed, table, kitchen, telephone. These, along with the rusting F-reg van outside, were the entire visible assets of Duffy Security after its initial operating period of six years. It didn't bother Duffy: the less you had, the easier it was to keep tidy. It might have bothered a few clients, but they never actually got to visit the 'offices' of Duffy Security. Duffy explained the condition of his van – if he caught one of those looks which said, 'Why did I pick *you* out of the Yellow Pages?' – by saying that it made surveillance work easier. Any wally can buy himself a new motor and put it against tax, Duffy would add confidently. In his early days he would sometimes joke, when the clients seemed unimpressed by his van, that he was still saving up for the dog. He soon found out that clients didn't like jokes. They also, in a funny sort of way, wanted dogs. Duffy didn't want a dog. Dogs bit. Dogs worried Duffy.

Other things worried him more.

'Can you look at me back?'

'Nnn?' Carol was only half-awake. It was eight o'clock on a Sunday morning and she'd come off duty at two.

'I've looked at me legs, can you look at me back?'

Carol slowly opened her eyes and looked him up and down from shoulders to bum. 'It's all still there, Duffy, it hasn't run away.'

'Does it look the same?'

Carol squinted again, as carefully as the time of day allowed.

'You've got hair on your shoulderblades, Duffy, did you know that?'

'All the same otherwise?'

'It's disgusting, you know, Duffy.'

'What is?' Christ, had she spotted something?

'I should shave it off if I were you. It isn't a bit sexy.' Oh, that. 'I wouldn't mind doing it for you, Duffy. I mean, it's never going to be a feature.'

Duffy had gone back to sleep; Carol too, but less easily.

Over breakfast that morning he suddenly said to her, 'Do you know where to look for lymph nodes?'

'Some sort of cereal, are they, Duffy?'

He'd scowled a bit, and got on with his muesli. Carol knew it never did any good asking. Either he'd tell you, or he wouldn't tell you. Perhaps it was something to do with his football. He liked to start fretting quite early before a match.

'You be here when I get back?'

'Don't think so, Duffy. Stuff to do.'

'I see.' He knew not to ask things as well. Sometimes, they seemed to spend their time not asking. He looked across at the pretty, dark, Irish morning face of WPC Carol Lucas, and thought how even after all these years it was something nice to see in the mornings. He didn't tell her that, either. 'Only, you see, I thought we might ... do something.'

Do something? What did he mean? They never did anything. When had they last done anything? That Greek meal the previous summer? Or had he taken her for a drive in the van since – yes, that time when he had something worth nicking in the back, and one of the door locks didn't work, and he'd had to see a client on the way to somewhere else. Carol had sat in the van guarding a cardboard box containing she didn't know what for half an hour. That was the last time they'd 'done something'.

Her friends assumed they didn't go out much because they were always in bed. She'd told them Duffy did a bit of weight-training (well, he had a couple of dumb-bell things too heavy for her to lift which he kept in the fitted cupboard in the bedroom) and they'd jumped to the obvious conclusions. 'Pumping iron again, last night, was it?' they'd sometimes ask. That was very far from being it, but Carol always smiled. She and Duffy had held the world chastity record for – what? Five years? It didn't bear thinking about. Odd that she could still go for him, she thought. Odd that he still wanted her around. When that terrible thing had got him thrown out of the Force, when they'd framed him with that black kid who claimed to be under-age, he'd stopped being able to get it together with her. Tried everything for a bit, but no good. That would have been it for most people; but in a funny way they'd stuck together. Only by not asking a lot of questions, though.

'I could come back tomorrow if you like,' she offered.

'I've got a new dish I heat up in the oven.'

'That sounds smashing, Duffy. I'll put on my best dress.'

As he drove to the game, though, he started worrying if Carol had looked properly. Little brown irregular blotches, that was what he had read. Duffy shuddered. It had a nasty name, too. Kaposi's sarcoma. That didn't sound like something you got better from. Who the hell was this Kaposi guy? He had a name like one of those old Hollywood movie stars. Bela Kaposi.

Of course, there was nothing to show that he'd got it. But on the other hand there was nothing to show that he hadn't got it. This didn't strike Duffy as a very good deal.

At first, it had just been a scare story in the papers, KILLER PLAGUE HITS US GAYS. One of those things they have over there, he thought, like Legionnaire's Disease, WHAT KILLED GAY PLAGUE MAN? Over-indulgence, Duffy thought, as he read the headline and passed on. US CHRISTIANS SAY GOD IS PUNISHING GAYS. And so it continued, NO HELP YET FOR AIDS VICTIMS. Then: SHOULD GAYS CHANGE THEIR LIFESTYLE? And finally, dreadfully, one morning: KILLER GAY PLAGUE AIDS IS HERE.

Duffy soon learnt what the initials stood for. Acquired Immune Deficiency Syndrome. Attacks Homosexuals, Heroin Addicts, Haitians and Haemophiliacs. Everyone with an H in their name: like only eating shellfish when there's an R in the month, or something. Homosexual includes Bisexual, Duffy read. Duffy had been pretty bisexual in his time. Well, all that would have to stop. If he'd picked it up, though, everything would stop. Everything. One hundred per cent death-rate after three years or so for all diagnosed cases. No way of knowing whether you were going to get it, no way of knowing whether you'd already got it, and no cure.

Promiscuous homosexuals especially at risk. Passive homosexuals especially at risk. Well, of course he'd been promiscuous. He'd also been promiscuous with women – did that help in any way? He'd been very promiscuous after things had all gone wrong with Carol; in fact he'd made a rule only to have one-night stands, because he didn't want to get involved. He also wanted to hang on to Carol, and having nothing but one-night stands, however many of them, was in a funny way being loyal to Carol. Not many other people would probably see it that way, but Duffy did. He'd had a year or two of being, yes, well, up for anything that moved, really. Then it sort of settled down, and he was just averagely promiscuous now. He didn't necessarily keep to his one-night-only rule, because he didn't feel his relationship with Carol was under threat any more. At least not from his side. Her side was another matter. He didn't like to think about that.

Passive homosexuals especially at risk. No comment, Duffy muttered to himself.

First you get infected, they said. Someone who's been on a package tour to San Francisco; a tasty American who's found the Alligator Club in his *Spartacus Gay Guide to the World* and dropped in for a trawl. Then nothing happens. That was the scary bit. Nothing happens for six months or so. Then you feel a bit unwell, you get night sweats, lose a little weight, get the runs, have a high temperature; and these lymph node things swell up.

That'll go on for a bit – perhaps as much as a year – and suddenly it goes away. Completely. You feel fine. Never better. Back down the Alligator and no problem. The only problem is, your entire immunity system has been wiped out. No resistance left: a common cold blows you away, or some odd form of pneumonia. Or, most likely of all, this Bela Kaposi comes along with the old sarcoma, and the brown blotches start, and that's it. You might as well put your head in a polythene bag and save the National Health Service some money.

Had he felt unwell in the last year or so? Of course he had. Of course he sometimes woke up sweating in the night; who didn't? Temperature? Occasionally. Weight-loss? Yes, but he thought that was a good thing at the time; he didn't want to get fat, so he'd started pumping iron and watching his diet. Bit of a health-food kick, almost. Diarrhoea? Who doesn't find himself doubling back to the toilet once in a while? You don't keep a record, though, do you?

Or on the other hand he could still be in the six-month incubation period. The first cases in Britain were only just being officially confirmed. But by 'cases' they meant deaths. And these 'cases' wouldn't have lived their last couple of years any differently from how they'd lived the earlier ones. So think of all those six-month incubation periods stacked up one behind the other, waiting to burst out. No wonder people were getting so jumpy down at the clubs. No wonder anyone with an American accent couldn't even get a drink. Duffy still called in at the Alligator; there wasn't any reason to boycott the place – it wasn't as if they put AIDS in the beer there, though some people behaved as if they did. But he always went home alone, nowadays.

No more men. Not for a bit. Watch out for night sweats. Try and find out where your lymph nodes are.

It wasn't Duffy's brightest game for the Reliables that Sunday. He missed a punch on a corner: one–nil. He came out far too late when the back four was caught square: two–nil. He got an elbow in the side at a free kick and was too winded to see who'd done it. And he ended up being scooted round by a fat midfielder who picked the ball out of the net for him, and proudly announced that it was his first goal in eighteen months: three–nil.

He didn't feel too bright in the shower afterwards, either. There had been times when he would glance around the flesh on display and have a quiet smile to himself. Pity they're all *straight*, he'd think. Now he half-closed his eyes as the shorts were dropped, and winced as all these pink, healthy, heterosexual bums came waltzing confidently out of the shower. Herpes was the most they'd be worrying about.

One of the bums belonged to Ken Marriott – Maggot, as he was affectionately known to the team, because of the way he kept getting under opponents' skins. There was something about Maggot that really riled other outfits. Probably the way he kicked them; they never did seem to get used to that. Maggot was tall and thin and bad-tempered-looking, and didn't have much hair left: most of it had been worn off on all those strikers he'd butted. But then, if he hadn't been a touch on the physical side, he probably wouldn't have kept his place with the Reliables. For Ken suffered from a terrible affliction: he was a thinker. He worked on the sports desk of the *West London Chronicle*; perhaps that was where he got his ideas. He talked a lot about 'vision', and 'changing the point of attack', and 'spreading the ball wide'.

'He's got great vision, our Maggot,' said Karl French after one match. Karl French was the fittest, youngest and smartest member of the Reliables, and they were lucky to get him. 'Great vision. Only trouble is, the ball doesn't go *anywhere fucking near* where he wants it to.'

Maggot was always trying to play subtle chips round the edge of the box, or back-heel the ball at speed, or lay it off one-touch with a caress of the boot. The Reliables forgave him these delusions of grandeur because of his defensive qualities. He could mistime a tackle like no one else in the team; and since he was tall and thin and looked a bit uncoordinated, the ref often let him get away with it.

'I know I'm a bit rugged,' Marriott had once explained, almost apologetically, after an especially vicious game, 'but I've got this vision as well, you see.'

'Course you've got vision, Maggot,' said French consolingly. 'Anyone can see that. Great vision. It's just a question of whether the rest of us can adapt our game to fit in with you.'

Maggot thought he had made a friend for life.

As they were leaving the ground, Marriott asked Duffy for a lift back. Despite his vision, he'd so far been unable to persuade any driving-test examiner to allow him on the road unaccompanied.

'Been seeing a bit of Jimmy Lister lately,' he began, as he untangled his seat belt.

'Uh-huh.'

'Now there's a man with problems.'

'Uh-huh.' Not like mine, thought Duffy. Bet Jimmy Lister doesn't get night sweats. Or if he does, they're only about something short-term, like losing his job.

'Ever met him?'

'No. Liked him as a player. Bit of a berk as a manager, isn't he?'

'You try managing Athletic with Melvyn Prosser breathing down your neck.'

'What's he earn? Fifteen thou? Twenty?'

'Something like, I should think.'

'Well, I'd let Melvyn Prosser breathe down my neck for that money.'

'Pressure, Duffy. That job's all about pressure.'

'Why does he wear white shoes if he isn't a berk?' said Duffy aggressively. He had more things to worry about than Jimmy Lister's employment prospects. They drove on in silence for a bit.

'How's business, Duffy?'

'All right.'

'Good.'

'It's all right.'

'Turning down work?'

'Not exactly.'

'Want a job?'

'Thought you'd never ask.'

'Ah.'

'What is it? Nannying the rest of Lister's mob so they don't all go on the piss and get themselves into fights?'

'Anyone would think you didn't want work, from the fuss you make.'

Duffy grunted. Maybe he should pack it in and take it easy for the last couple of years or so of his life. Perhaps he'd marry Carol on his deathbed at the hospital. Except that he might not even get admitted to the hospital. He'd read about some doctors and nurses refusing to treat AIDS victims. Too dangerous. Not enough known about the way the disease spreads. Filthy queers, anyway. Duffy wouldn't be surprised if, by the time he got his Kaposi thing, all the guys with AIDS were being packed off to some leper colony in the Welsh mountains. Made to wear little bells round their necks so people could hear them coming. Ding-dong, ding-dong. No, dear, that's not the ice-cream van, it's the man with AIDS come to dig in our dustbins. *Do* go and turn the hose on him again, will you? Or why not just shoot him this time, darling.

Jimmy Lister was wearing black shoes. He was also wearing a polo-neck sweater and an old pair of jeans. Obviously Miss West London wasn't going to come and sit on his knee for the benefit of the press this morning. He'd filled out a bit since Duffy had last watched him from the terraces; but you could see the remains of a lean, elegant player of the sort that Maggot deludedly supposed himself to be. Above his ears a few bits of sandy hair were still left. He got up, smiled and shook hands with Duffy, who found himself thinking, Maybe you aren't a berk after all.

'Ken Marriott told me you ... looked after things.'
'I'm not a minder.'
'No. I mean, you looked *into* things.'
'That's more like it.'
'Call me Jimmy.'
'All right.'
'What shall I call you?'
'What do you want me to look into?'
Lister glanced across at Duffy. I'm not surprised you don't get too much work, my lad, if this is how you go about it. Where are the customer relations? What about a little smile? Fat chance of that, he could see. Duffy had a small, tight mouth set in a broad face, and it moved

only to speak. His hair looked as if it had once been in a brush-cut, and then had been allowed to fend for itself.

'You follow Athletic much?'

'No.'

'Any particular reason?' Jimmy didn't mind going in for a bit of customer relations, even if this strange chum of Marriott's didn't.

Duffy thought about this one for a moment; Lister was almost on tenterhooks.

'I don't think they're much good, that's why.'

'Charming.'

'Anyway, QPR's my team.'

'QPR? With that nancy-boy pitch of theirs?'

'Fifty quid a day, plus exes,' was all Duffy said to this. He put his thumb to his left earlobe, felt the ridged scar and rubbed it. He had worn a gold stud in that ear until one day someone had done something nasty to it. He was still debating whether or not to have his right ear pierced and start again. The chances of the same thing happening twice were pretty thin; but then the chances of having your earlobe being nearly torn off in the first place by a maniac with a pair of pliers aren't exactly high, are they?

'You read about Danny—'

'Fifty a day, plus exes.'

'Sure, sure. I'll have to clear it with the chairman, but I reckon it'll be OK. You read about Danny Matson?'

'Uh-huh.'

'What did you think?'

'I didn't think. I wasn't being paid to.'

'Look, er, Mr Duffy ...'

'Duffy.'

'Duffy, thank you.' So he did answer questions eventually. 'What I thought at first was, he got himself into a fight. Maximum he got mugged. Extreme maximum some of those Barnsley fans were still hanging around for some reason and decided to work him over. I mean, they need the points as badly as us.'

'Is he out of the game for long?'

'For good, I'd say. At this level. Bit of Southern League stuff left in him if he's lucky. He's only twenty.'

'Poor sod.' Even so, that still left him with an average life expectancy of another fifty years; he had that to look forward to. 'But now you don't think he got mugged?'

'Well, this isn't the smartest end of town, I know. But if it was a fight, if he was trying to kick out, he wouldn't kick out backwards, would he?'

'Not unless he was a horse.'

'Quite. I think someone did Danny.'

'What changed your mind?'

'Several things. Partly this.' Lister reached into his desk and fetched out some long papers, folded in half vertically. 'It's a writ. Or rather, it's three writs.'

'You need a lawyer.'

'Thanks. I'd never have guessed. It's three writs. All from people living in Layton Road. Sueing the club for persistent trespass by our loyal fans, various amounts of damage by the same loyal fans stretching back over a period of years, and applying to the court to get the Layton Road entrance closed on match days.'

'Is that bad?'

'The first two bits aren't so bad. We don't mind paying out a bit to keep the locals sweet. Customer relations, it's called, Duffy.'

'Never heard of it.'

'The Layton Road entrance, as you might not know, being a supporter of the wrong team, is where all our bad

33

boys go in. So that they can shout rude things from the Piggeries end.'

'How bad are your bad boys?'

'About as bad as you can get.'

'It's not like that at QPR.'

'Really? I suppose all your bad boys just sing nursery rhymes, applaud the referee, and line up for fingernail inspection afterwards?'

Duffy grinned. 'That's about it. Nice family club, QPR. So anyway?'

'So if home and away fans have to go in at the same entrance, there's bound to be a bit more aggravation, isn't there?'

'Still, if I lived in Layton Road and had to put up with all your bad boys, I'd have done the same myself before now.'

'Point taken. But why now? It's not as if it's the start of the season. There's only half a dozen home matches left.'

'Hmm. Anything else?'

'You seen one of these before?'

Lister passed him a crudely printed handbill. It read:

WANTED!

ARE YOU YOUNG? ARE YOU STRONG?
ARE YOU BRITISH?
ARE YOU FED UP WITH THE WAY
THIS COUNTRY HAS GONE SOFT?
ARE YOU FED UP WITH THE WAY
THIS COUNTRY IS PUSHED AROUND?
DO YOU THINK THE RACES CAN
LIVE SIDE BY SIDE?

> DO YOU BELIEVE IN REPATRIATION?
> ORGANISE!
> STRENGTH WILL WIN!
> JOIN THE RED WHITE AND BLUE
> MOVEMENT!

'Never had any of this stuff down here before,' said Lister. 'At least, that's what the physio says, and he's been here for years. Never anything like that.'

'Not very nice,' said Duffy, after reading it and looking in vain for a printer's name at the bottom. 'How long have they been dishing these out?'

'No idea,' said Lister. 'Weeks, months? They made the mistake of giving one to some student the other Saturday; he sent it in to us. Said he felt a bit relieved he'd left off his Anti-Nazi League badge for the afternoon.'

'What's it got to do with football?'

'In theory, nothing. We don't mind how many whackos we let in through the turnstiles as long as they pay their money. And as long as they behave themselves.'

'These don't?'

'Not sure. Don't know how long they've been handing these things out.'

'What's the Red White and Blue Movement?'

'Never heard of it. But I remember something similar down at Millwall a year or two ago. What happens is that these, what do you call them, neo-Nazis or whatever, start using the grounds as recruiting centres. Wanted – Big strong white men to beat up small brown men: that's about what this says, isn't it?'

'More or less.'

'So the Nazis recruit the thugs, and the thugs all

35

watch the football together, and the thugs go to the Nazi rallies, and bring more thugs along to watch the football. And the thugs drive away the fans. Why should anyone come along here and pay a couple of quid to stand in the rain and see his side lose and then get spat at by some fourteen-year-old skinhead as he's leaving the ground?'

'It doesn't happen at QPR,' said Duffy.

'Well it's not going to bloody happen here. I don't train a team to play in front of a crowd of yobbos who might or might not give us a passing glance when they take a breather from stabbing one another and ripping the safety barriers apart.'

'I see the point, er, Jimmy. But it's a little long-term, isn't it?' Lister, he thought, was clearly a worrier.

'I'll give you the short-term, then. The news hasn't exactly crept into the papers yet, and it's your friend and mine Ken Marriott who's helping keep it out at the moment. But there've been quite a lot more fights at the last few home matches. Quite a bit more boot than usual. Now what this means is, more policemen. I don't know if you know much about how the police work—'

'Not much.'

'—but they don't just turn up to our matches out of the kindness of their hearts and because they want to see a good game of football. For a start, this is private property, and we have to invite them in to get them. Second, we have to have a weekly conference about how much work we think we're going to give them. And third, we have to pay them. Saturday afternoon is overtime rates, as well.'

Duffy remembered all too well. Pulled out of his Saturday rest day and bussed up to north London. However much you frisked the thugs, they still managed to find things to throw at you. Once, he was in a line of eight coppers – eight neat helmets standing in a row – when someone on the terraces had heaved half a brick at them. As it whizzed through the air, about a hundred friendly supporters started chanting, 'Coconut! Coconut!' He hadn't thought much to those Saturday afternoons.

'So more thugs means more fights means more police means more money. Closing Layton Road means more fights means more police means more money. And there's another thing. They've started booing big Brendan.'

'Brendan Domingo?'

'Yup. Never happened before. He's used to being booed at away games, that's normal. But he's been in the team for nearly two seasons now, and always been popular at home. Now the Layton Road end has started booing him.'

'Is he out of form?'

'Brendan? He's playing like a dream. Never better. That spell of a dozen games with Danny really sparked him. Lovely control. Silky skills. He's our best player now. Whether he'll stay like that if the Layton Road end keeps it up ... It's very demoralising, Duffy, being booed by your own supporters. Makes you wonder why you should give a monkey's.'

'I know.' Duffy had been booed one Sunday by the entire Reliables supporters' club; both of them.

'I mean, if *I* were him, I wouldn't give a monkey's.' Lister sighed. He was looking worried again. Duffy decided to sum up.

'You think someone's out to get you, don't you? The club, that is.'

'I think I do.'

'So what you want me to do is find out who clobbered Danny Matson, find out why the Layton Road residents

37

are suddenly cutting up rough, stop the neo-Nazis gathering at home matches, stop the thugs booing Brendan Domingo, stop Brendan Domingo losing his form, save you from relegation – and help you keep your job.'

'Sounds as if you've got your hands full.'

'I'm saving up for a dog,' Duffy threw in light-heartedly, and immediately regretted it. Shit, why did he say that? Why had it slipped out again? He thought Jimmy Lister had a sense of humour. Listen, Duffy, *no* client has a sense of humour, remember? Even if he laughs a lot.

'Any questions?'

'Well, I'd like to meet the chairman.'

'He's not in till the day after tomorrow. I suppose he might see you at his headquarters if you asked nicely, though.'

'Thanks. No, that'll do for the moment.'

They got up, and Lister showed him towards the door. Duffy noticed that there weren't any cups or trophies in the office. Nothing silver at all. Perhaps all that stuff was kept in the boardroom. Or perhaps Athletic had never won anything.

'You play in goal, I hear?'

'Uh-huh. You don't happen to know where your lymph nodes are, do you?'

'No idea. Ask the physio.'

'Right.'

They shook hands. 'Oh, er, Jimmy?'

'Yes?'

'Why aren't you wearing the white shoes?'

'I'm not a berk, Duffy.'

'Right.'

*

Danny Matson was sitting in a purple armchair with his leg up on a footstool. A copy of the *Sun* had been placed on the stool so that his plaster cast wouldn't mess it up. Mrs Ferris kept a clean set of digs; always had, since she'd started taking in boys for Athletic a dozen years ago. The club liked to look after its players. The best way of looking after them, of course, was to see that they got married. A player needed stability, the club always said: all that rushing around and adulation, best thing for him is a nice wife at home, a couple of toddlers, a car to take down the car-wash and a garage to paint in the winter. Stops them losing their heads, stops them taking to the booze and the birds too much (mind you, even the married ones got a bit naughty sometimes: take them off on a pre-season friendly tour to some hot country and you wouldn't believe the high jinks). But you couldn't force them to get married; so until that time the club liked to put them in reliable digs with careful, motherly ladies who were always given a pair of free tickets to the home games. They weren't there to spy on the lads; they were there to look after them; though, of course, if one of the boys was having a bit of trouble that the landlady thought the club ought to know about, then they'd be more than grateful for a quiet hint on the side. Who wouldn't be?

The club liked to lodge the lads in pairs. 'The animals came in two by two,' as Mrs Ferris would tend to shout out from her kitchen when her couple of boys had some trouble with the front door after a hard Saturday night on the Bacardi. The boys were company for one another; they talked about the game a bit, and it was surprising how often their understanding on the park improved if they roomed together. Danny Matson roomed with Brendan

Domingo. When Duffy called, Brendan was out: down at the ground doing his sprints, lifting his weights, trying one-touch stuff with the player they'd brought in to replace Danny, practising corners and free kicks, or simply off at one end of the pitch by himself improving his silky skills. Danny sat with his big white foot up on a copy of the *Sun* and waited for Brendan to come home. The whole business really rather pissed him off.

He looked a slight lad to Duffy: pale, long face, with black hair in a curly perm that was just beginning to grow out. Footballers always looked a little smaller off the pitch; this one was no exception. He waited for Duffy's questions with politeness – the Boss had phoned ahead and asked him to cooperate in any way he could – but a sort of cheerful boredom. He didn't care any more who had done his leg. It was done, wasn't it? Snapped. Danny thought of all the players who'd had Achilles trouble. They were never quite the same again, even if they were still good. Look at Trevor Francis. Blistering speed he used to have; blistering. Then the trouble, and the lay-off, and at least a yard of pace had gone by the time he came back. Still a fine player, in Danny's view – don't get me wrong, still a fine player – but not world class any more. Not world class.

They went through the incident in the car-park; the police had already done that with him a few times. Duffy asked if there was any detail he might have forgotten; then asked him a lot about the girl who'd picked him up, or who he'd picked up (the precise order of things was still a bit blurry). Did the men say anything? How long did it take to walk from The Knight Spot to the car-park? Who was on duty at the payout? And so on.

'If you don't mind my saying, mister, I've been asked these questions before.'

'Well, there might be something you've forgotten. Some little detail. That's why I'm asking them again.'

'But the coppers have already done that. Asked it once, then sent someone else back a bit later in case there was anything I'd forgotten.'

'Well, third time lucky, perhaps.'

But it wasn't third time lucky. The men hadn't said anything; he hadn't seen their faces; they hadn't taken anything more than his wallet and his watch; no, he couldn't remember anything more about this Denise girl. Black hair, he'd said, black dress and showing quite a lot. Sure he'd liked her; but that didn't mean he could remember much about her. Sure he'd recognise her if he saw her again, he wasn't thick.

'Danny, I wonder if you'd do something for me. I wonder if you'd go down The Knight Spot with me one evening and have a look for her.'

'Well, that's very smart thinking, if I may say so, Mr Duffy, but you see I've already done that with the coppers. Twice. And she wasn't there.'

This didn't surprise Duffy too much. He was only an ex-copper himself: he was bound to do some things the same way as the coppers. Neither did the girl's disappearance surprise him: if she'd been genuine, and really was a nice ordinary girl, she'd probably have got in touch with Danny. The attack had been in all the papers. Why hadn't she dropped him a line saying she was sorry she hadn't waited but it had been perishing cold, and she was sorry about his accident, and maybe she could pop round in her nurse's outfit and ruffle his hair? But on the other hand, the fact that she hadn't written didn't necessarily make her a phoney. Perhaps she just liked her footballers all in one piece.

'I expect you'll be going to see Vince,' said Danny.

'Who's Vince?'

'Vince runs The Knight Spot.'

'Right.'

'And Fat Frankie?'

'Who's Fat Frankie?'

'Fat Frankie's the bouncer.'

'Expect so.'

'Well, Fat Frankie can't remember one person going out of the club from the next. Not unless they make trouble. Plus which, he's got a bit of a lager problem. Vince didn't even see me with a girl all evening.'

'How do you know?'

'The coppers checked it all out. How else?'

'Danny, will you come down The Knight Spot with me once more?'

'No. No. Look, I'd like to help, obviously. But … the plain fact is I promised myself I wouldn't go back, not till I was in the first team again. It made me feel bloody awful going down there with the coppers, I don't mind telling you. Going in on bloody crutches, seeing all those people dancing. I even ran into one of the lads.'

'Yeah, I see.'

'I mean, it's not like I got this going for a fifty-fifty ball or something. I'd just be sitting there in plaster and they wouldn't be thinking, "Oh look, isn't that Danny Matson up there, pity about the injury, brave lad isn't he, wonder how long he'll be out, why don't we buy him a drink and cheer him up?" No, it wouldn't be that, it'd be, "Look at that Matson kid over there, what a wally, gets

42

himself pissed and beaten up just when the team needed him most, makes you sick, doesn't it?"'

That's probably what they would be thinking, Duffy silently agreed. But Danny was a willing lad – apart from anything else he seemed glad of company – and eventually they struck a compromise. Duffy would pick him up one evening; they'd park outside The Knight Spot and just watch the customers going in. Danny thought he could handle that; and the Boss had asked him to cooperate as best he could.

'You follow the game much, Mr Duffy?'

'A bit. QPR's my team, though.'

'Ah well, now, QPR. Don't let the Boss catch me saying it, but QPR's a classy outfit. Classy.'

Duffy nodded. They lapsed into silence.

'It's a funny old game, Mr Duffy, isn't it?' Duffy agreed. 'I mean, I haven't been in it long, not really in it, not at first-team level, but already it's taught me a thing or two.' Duffy nodded. 'It can be a very kind game, Mr Duffy, it can give you lots of things.' Duffy nodded again. 'And it can be a very cruel game. It can build you up; and then it can knock you down. It's a bit like life, really, isn't it?'

Duffy concurred.

'Have a feel in that pocket over there.' Danny was pointing to his blazer, which hung on the back of the door. Duffy reached in and pulled out a square of slightly shiny paper. On a nod from Danny he unfolded it and laid the two pages side by side. Spread across most of them was a large photograph of a sitting room. Crouched in the middle of a huge area of brightly patterned carpet was a smiling, dark-haired man holding a small child. The child was half-balanced, rather precariously, on a football.

'That's Trevor Brooking's room,' said Danny. 'I got it out of one of the posh Sundays.'

Duffy examined the photograph. He saw a couple of large wooden cabinets, mostly full of silverware; a large yellow leather armchair, matching a large yellow leather sofa; a carved fireplace; a low glass-topped coffee-table.

'Very nice,' he said.

'That's Warren. With Trevor. He's nearly four. Well, he was nearly four when the photo was taken. I suppose he's a bit bigger now. And there's Colette, she was seven. And there's Hilke, she's Finnish. That's Trevor's wife. Hilke keeps the place really tidy, it says.'

'Very nice.' Duffy liked the sound of Hilke.

'Look at the picture Trevor's got over the fireplace.' Duffy could just make out a gold frame; inside it, a family, standing somewhere.

'That's Trevor getting his MBE at Buckingham Palace. With Hilke, and Warren, and Colette. They have this photographer standing outside, and he takes the picture, and then you have it framed.'

'Nice.'

'Do you see the decanters? And look at that fireplace. It's not a real fireplace, actually, there isn't a chimney, but Trevor likes fireplaces so he had it put in. It's electric.'

'Nnn.'

'And look at the way the stereo's built in. That must have cost a bomb. And the chess set. And the candlesticks on the coffee-table. I bet they're real silver.'

'It's a very nice room, Danny.'

'His wife's Finnish. She's called Hilke.'

'Very nice.'

'He's one of the all-time greats, Trevor Brooking, don't you think?'

'No question.' Duffy refolded the pages carefully. 'Better be on my rounds, Danny. Might call back sometime if that's all right?'

'Sure. Any time. One thing I can't work out – do you think the room's really as big as that, or do you think they took the photo with one of those wide-angle lenses?'

Duffy unfolded the pages again.

'It's hard to tell.'

He turned to go. It was only about four feet from the middle of the room to the door. If ever they came to do Danny Matson's room, they'd certainly need a wide-angle lens.

Three phone calls. The first to Jimmy Lister, asking what the club's policy was on the Layton Road residents.

'Delay, Duffy. Delay the case as long as possible. I mean, it's coming up in court this Friday, so they can try and close the gates for Saturday. But even if it goes against us, we can try appealing, or whatever.'

'Has anyone been down to talk to the residents?'

'No. We thought about it. But we decided the best way of making sure everything happens as slowly as possible was to do it through solicitors. Then if it all works out in the end we'll bung them a few free tickets, something like that.'

'What about the press?'

'Complete news blackout, that's our policy on the press, Duffy.'

'No one been sniffing around?'

'No one.'

The second call. To Ken Marriott at the *Chronicle*.

'Ken, if I asked you whether or not you'd heard a

particular story and you hadn't, that wouldn't necessarily be the same as me telling you the story, would it?'

'How do you mean?'

'I mean, you could hold off for a day or two, and pretend I'd told you later, couldn't you?'

'I suppose so. It'd depend a bit on copy day, and what the story was. This week – this week I could give you forty-eight hours easily. Unless there's a lot of work to do on the story.'

'Did you know about Athletic being sued by local residents?'

'No. Interesting. Which residents? Where? What for?'

'Forty-eight hours?'

'As long as you come back to me and no one else.'

'Right.'

Third call. To the Anti-Nazi League.

'Oh, it's Ken Marriott of the *West London Chronicle*. *West London Chronicle*. Wondered if you can help us. We're doing a story about neo-Nazis recruiting at football matches. We think it might be starting up at the Athletic ground – some outfit called the Red White and Blue Movement. Just wondered if you had any information on them?'

They had, it seemed, more than enough information on the Red White and Blue Movement. Especially about its affiliation to other, similar groups, most of whom Duffy had never heard of, and about its exact political position, which sounded pretty nasty, and about its organising members, their backgrounds and criminal records. It was an impressive dossier, and Duffy pretended to be taking it all down. What he mainly wanted to ask, though, was how long the Movement had been in existence, and where it operated from. Six months, and an address in

46

Ealing were the answers. Duffy offered fraternal thanks, and rang off.

Layton Road consisted of two low terraces of red-brick Victorian villas. They were neatly kept; some of them had been freshly painted. It looked a houseproud little street. Duffy approved. He took out a notebook and started at number 37.

'Oh, good morning, sir—'

'No.'

'But I'm—'

'No samples, no religions,' the man said. He was small and fierce, with crinkly grey hair and a jutting chin; he looked like a retired PT instructor.

'I'm from the *Chronicle*. The *West London Chronicle*.' At least that stopped the door being shut in his face; just.

'Oh yes.'

'Yes, Mr – Mr …' Duffy pretended to search his notebook for the name.

'What do you want?'

'Sorry to hear about the trouble you've been having.'

'How did you hear about it?'

'That's what we're paid to do.'

'Snoopers,' said the man. Duffy didn't feel he was getting anywhere. Suddenly the door was opened wide, the PT instructor came out, took him by the arm and marched him the four yards to the gate. Oh well, all in a reporter's day, he reflected. When they got there, however, the fellow kept hold of Duffy's arm and pushed him gently against the gate.

'Bullivant,' he said, answering a much earlier question. 'Look at it,' he went on, pointing at the street. 'Nice, isn't it? Nice little houses. Very clean, very quiet. See all these cars? Nice cars. Every home game we have to move them quarter of a mile away. Freer access for the crowds, that's what the police say. Stop them getting vandalised by the yobbos, that's the truth of it. Look at these front gardens. Notice anything odd about them? Nothing in them. Just hedges, nothing else. No flowers, no plants. No point having flowers, the yobbos just pull them up. No point having window boxes, the yobbos knock them off. No point *chaining* your window boxes to your window sills, that just excites them some more. Animals.'

'Can you tell me why you haven't complained before?'

'Have complained before. Makes no bloody difference. All they do is send you a couple of free tickets for the next match. Who wants free tickets to watch a bloody awful side like Athletic? Send me free tickets to go and watch Tottenham and you're talking. Anyway, the only time I feel happy about those yobbos is when they're all locked up inside the ground making their animal noises. What on earth makes the club think I want to go inside as well and listen to their obscene chantings from a bit nearer?

'Ever had a chicken takeaway through your door? Course you haven't. Disgusting food. Even the dog wouldn't eat it. Ever had a yobbo doing his ablutions through your letter box? Course you haven't. Ever had a yobbo doing his business in your front garden? Course you haven't. You don't know what's going on, my lad, you with your sharp pencil and big fat notebook and not writing anything down in it I see. You just don't know what's going on. You know another thing they like doing. They like ringing on the door and asking if they can use the toilet. Course you can't, you say, use the one at the ground, and you close the door on them and there's a bloody great explosion. Know what they've done? They've stuck a lightbulb in the door just as you're closing it. Done that twice to me. Great sense of fun, the yobbos. Then they do their ablutions in your front garden because you wouldn't let them use the toilet. Haven't got any free tickets for Tottenham on you by any chance, have you, my lad? No, I thought not. Good morning to you.'

And Mr Bullivant marched back up his path and slammed the door.

Duffy crossed the road to number 48. The door was opened a couple of inches, as far as the chain would permit. 'Arthur's not in.'

'Good morning, madam, I'm from the *Chronicle*. I was talking to Mr Bullivant—'

'Arthur's not in.'

'Could I talk to you instead?'

'He'll be back later.'

'When would be a good time to call?'

'Not now.'

'Thank you for your help.'

At number 57 a red-faced lady in a tight perm and a pinafore answered the door.

'Oh, the *Chronicle*. Very nice. Always read it. If I'd known you was coming I'd have taken off me pinny. Will you be wanting a photograph?'

'Er, not today perhaps.'

'Oh, be sending him round later, will you? That'll give me time to get tidied up. But you'll be the one with the cheque?'

'I'm sorry?'

'You mean I haven't won the Lucky Numbers? No, I can see I haven't. Oh well, another fortune slips through my fingers.' She looked quite cheerful about it.

'No, it's about the trouble with the fans, Mrs …'

'Davis. That's D-A-V-I-S. Right.' She leaned over Duffy's arm while he recorded the first piece of information to enter his notebook. 'Yes, that's right, without an E. No, I don't really mind them myself. They're not bad lads. Not really wicked, just a bit high-spirited. I mean, we were all young once, weren't we?'

Duffy thought he still was young. But perhaps it was a sign of middle age that you felt no inclination to stuff half-eaten takeaways through people's letter boxes. Yes, that must be it.

'I was just wondering why you all decided to go to law, especially as there are only a few home matches left in the season.'

Mrs Davis looked momentarily flustered, then gathered herself.

'I'm afraid my husband deals with all the bills. He earns the money, he gives me the housekeeping I need – he's a very fair man, my husband, don't you go thinking the contrary – and when the bills come in, he deals with them. Always keep a bit back for a rainy day, that's what he says, and he's quite right too.' Politely, she closed the door.

Duffy was puzzled. In one way, of course, it was all quite straightforward and understandable. The yobbos were getting worse and worse – Jimmy Lister had said they were fighting more on the terraces as well – and the residents had decided enough was enough. But *these* residents? If the yobbos were getting out of hand, they might go to the police. They might complain to the local paper. They might write to their local councillor, if they could remember who that was, or even to their MP. But going to a solicitor and having a writ served?

They might go to a solicitor to get divorced, or to make a will. But if someone like Mr Bullivant wanted to stop the yobbos doing their ablutions through his letter box, then he wouldn't go running to a solicitor. Someone like Mr Bullivant would be far more likely to get out his toolkit, file down the metal edge of his letter flap until it was really sharp, wait by his door until some heavily lagered boot-boy stuck his whatsit through the flap, and then *smack*. Very nasty too. Much nastier, and much more satisfying, than running to a pinstripe.

'I'm afraid Mr Prosser isn't too pleased,' said Jimmy Lister. Duffy had called in on his way to see the chairman. 'Not pleased at all. Thinks I'm way out of order hiring you, Duffy. Says he won't be putting this through the firm's books.'

'What does that mean?'

'It means that if I want you, I pay for you, Duffy.'

'So am I still in work?'

'Just. But I've done the calculations, and what I'd be paying you, Duffy, would be pretty much my entire salary; once the Taxman's been to call, that is. On top of which I'm currently into an alimony situation. Would you take thirty-five?'

'Oh all right.' Duffy thought he really must master this haggling business, one day.

'And you'll keep the expenses down?'

'No Concorde trips, I promise.'

'Just so we understand each other. Now I'll take you to meet Melvyn.'

Melvyn Prosser's boardroom was where they kept the club's silverware. One yellowing double-handled pot and a couple of shields. The pine-panelled walls of the large oblong room were covered with photographs: of the various Athletic teams down the years, and of the various Athletic Boards of Directors. The directors seemed to change as often as the teams and, in terms of wallspace, to be equally important.

Melvyn Prosser was standing by his desk in his camel-coloured overcoat giving a very decent impression of a busy man. Either he'd just arrived from somewhere, or he was just going somewhere; or perhaps he'd slipped on his overcoat especially for them, so that they'd realise how precious his time was. Having established the heavy suggestion of other priorities, Melvyn Prosser was prepared to be affable. He had a broad, fleshy face, with a vertical crease in the middle of his forehead which might possibly have been old scar tissue. It had been a quick climb, from blue collar to white collar to boardroom, and it couldn't have been achieved if Melvyn hadn't known how to smile while stamping on your fingers.

'James, welcome back. And Mr Duffy. Welcome. Sherry, beer? A pint of hooch, Mr Duffy, perhaps?' Duffy shook his head. It was quarter to eleven in the morning. 'Quite right. I'll abstain as well. Now James has told me about his curious decision to hire you, and as I expect you've heard, I very nearly said you may do the hiring, Jimmy, but I do the firing. Still, as the financial aspects have been sorted out I don't see any objection to you hanging around if you want to.'

'Thanks very—'

'Though I wouldn't mind being allowed to give you my view of the matters which Jimmy has doubtless already laid before you with a different emphasis.' Prosser gave a chairman's pause, the sort of pause which expects some sycophant to mumble, 'Go ahead, please, Mr Chairman.'

When none of this was instantly forthcoming, Prosser continued. 'I've heard what Jimmy's had to say and I'll tell you what I told him. I don't go in for conspiracy theories. I think we're chasing our own tails. I think *we* – that's a polite way of referring to my manager – are looking for excuses. I think *we* are in danger of losing our concentration on the matters in hand.'

'You don't think—'

'I would be as reluctant to criticise James as the next man, but I'm bound to say that he is in danger of looking for excuses. The club is not in the happiest of positions currently in the matter of League table position – in fact, if you'll pardon the phrase, it's all a bit dicky. But the way out of the maze is not to be found among the boot-boys on the terraces or among the residents of Layton Road. At least, that's my own ill-informed opinion. The way out of the maze is to be found on the park. Nowhere else. What I worry about is that our friend James's concentration on the matters in hand is in danger of going down the karzy, if you see what I mean.'

'You don't think anyone's trying to ...' Duffy wasn't quite sure how to put it.

'Trying to waggle the digit in the wrong orifice? Tell me who. Tell me why. Who cares if the club gets relegated? I do, Jimmy does, the Board does, the players and their wives do, and a few hundred of the older-style fans do. But why should anyone else care one way or another? I think we're in danger of looking for excuses, as I say. We're taking our minds off what really matters: how the players are playing. Jimmy's job, as I see it, is and always will be to do Jimmy's job.'

'Can I ask if you have any particular enemies, Mr Prosser?'

Prosser laughed, and then smiled a little patronisingly at Duffy.

'Did you see the car on the way in? Corniche, right? Gold Rolls-Royce Corniche, right? Now you don't get one of those in this society of ours without treading on a few toes, I'll give you that for nothing.'

'Anyone in particular?'

Prosser laughed again.

'Listen, if anyone was out to get *me*, they wouldn't do it through the club. It's nice having a club and all that, and believe me I'm committed to its future, but if I was the Big Bad Wolf out in the bushes looking to make it hot for Mel Prosser, I'd be going after some of his other business interests. Much easier. I wouldn't be bothered to start by duffing up his Davey Matsons.'

'Danny, chief.'

'Danny Matsons. How is the lad, Jimmy?'

'Bit down in the mouth, chief.'

'He's a good lad. Must be a bit of a blow, losing his first-team bonus.'

'But if,' Duffy persisted, 'there was someone ... some enemy – who would he be?'

'Vic Rivers, Solly Benson, Wally Mountjoy, Fiddler Mick, Steve Wilson, Charlie Magrudo, *Mrs* Charlie Magrudo, Dicky Jacks, Michael O'Brien, Tom Clancy, Stacky Stevenson, Reg Dyson ...' Prosser spread his hands. 'How many more do you want? My friends are my enemies. I like them, but I'd do them; same goes for them the other way round. I'm a businessman, do I make myself clear?'

'Anyone in particular?'

Prosser looked irritated. He looked as if he was being asked to squeal on a friend. He was, in a way.

'*Maybe* Charlie Magrudo. Maybe. I did him a bit of naughty a year or two ago.'

'What sort of naughty?'

'Not very naughty. Heard he was trying to line a few council pockets and fix himself up with a contract or two.' Melvyn smiled at the memory. 'So I dropped him in it and walked off with them myself. He didn't like it much. But I'm sure he's forgiven me by now.'

'Did he go down for it?'

'Go down? Good God no. I wouldn't do *that* to him. No, it was all kept within the old cream paint of the Town Hall. And then I got the contracts by laying out just half what Charlie had laid out. I liked that.'

Prosser turned his mind back to Duffy.

'And what have we found out so far that our friends in blue have missed? Any little leads? Giving young James his money's worth, I hope.'

'Not really. I'm trying to jog Danny Matson's memory. And I've been down Layton Road.'

'You've been down Layton Road? Harassing our residents and loyal supporters? That's a bit out of line, I'd say.'

'I wasn't harassing them. They were very cooperative.'

'Oh yes?'

'Yes, they wanted to tell me all about what the yobbos did through their letter boxes.'

'It's a terrible area, this,' said Prosser, hunching his shoulders in melodramatic resignation. 'Born and brought up within the sound of Sainsbury's supermarket, but it's sometimes hard to be loyal to it.'

'Mr Prosser, can I try out something else?'

Prosser checked his watch.

'You have three minutes and forty-five seconds.'

'Is the club making a profit?'

'You need to ask? No, the club is not making a profit, the club is making a healthy loss. It's the thing this club does most efficiently. James and I had various schemes at the beginning of the season with which we hoped to allure the paying customers, but I fear it was all pissing in the wind. We're lucky to get three thousand for a home game, and I'm afraid we're not one of the League's top attractions when we travel. What did we get at Rotherham? Under fifteen hundred, as I recall. No Cup run worth speaking of ...'

'Putting it bluntly, Mr Prosser, are you paying most of the bills out of your own pocket?'

'Answering it bluntly, Mr Duffy, yes I am.'

'Would the club be a viable proposition in the Fourth Division?'

'Duffy, those are words we do not utter anywhere on these premises, do you understand? No one, but no one, mentions those words.'

'Sorry. Sorry. But I was just ... Look, in the extremely unlikely event of ... of the worst coming to the worst, what would happen? I mean, what would actually happen?'

'Well, if a certain sad day in the history of this distinguished club were to come to pass, the first thing to happen is that Jim-boy here would be on his bike and looking into his career prospects. Sorry, Jimmy.'

'You've always been level with me, chief. I wouldn't expect anything else.'

'And then?' said Duffy.

'Then it would be a matter for the Board.'

'Or at least for its major shareholder.'

'Yes I am, as a matter of fact. Clever of you to guess. Well, yes, there would be various options to consider.'

'Any you'd care to share with us? Purely in the unlikely event of, naturally.'

'Naturally. Well, the chairman would have to resign.'

'Melvyn,' said Jimmy with genuine surprise. 'You couldn't ... Not after all you've done for the club.'

'James, let's not get sentimental. All I've done for the club in my two years as chairman is foot a not inconsiderable wages bill, redesign the players' strip, appoint you, preside over a four-figure decline in attendance, and watch us go down the table from tenth to twenty-second.'

'And what else?' asked Duffy.

'Are you always so persistently gloomy, Mr Duffy? What else? Well, I imagine the Board would go through the usual motions, there would be much wailing and gnashing of teeth, the playing staff would be reduced, the best players would be sold off, we might start looking for a cheap manager. Or we could just wind the whole thing up.'

'If the chief shareholder said so.'

'The chief shareholder would obviously have an influential say in the matter.'

'You couldn't do that, Melvyn,' said Jimmy protestingly. 'It's not as if we were bottom of the unmentionable and applying for re-election.'

'Times have changed, James. Times are hard. Every division has half a dozen clubs scraping along on the breadline, with some indulgent chairman holding them up by the bootstraps. Just because you aren't bottom of that division which we agree not to mention by name doesn't mean you're safe. Who's going to pay the wages? Where are they going to find another Melvyn Prosser from? I don't mind telling you I've tried looking around a bit in the last few months, and I reckon I've got about as much chance of unloading this club as I have of selling choc-ices to the Eskimos.' There was a silence. 'But I'd better be on my way, before I cheer you up some more. Still, what I've just said ought to persuade you of one thing, Mr Duffy.'

'You tell me.'

'That if there is a Big Bad Wolf out to get me, his best tactics are to make sure we avoid relegation so that I carry on being bled dry paying the bills for another year.'

'Point taken,' said Duffy, as Melvyn Prosser swept off for an appointment with his gold Rolls-Royce Corniche. Jimmy Lister was head down, and flattening his remnants of sandy hair with his fists. Duffy felt sorry for him. Eventually Jimmy stopped rubbing his head and spoke.

'Bit of a choker, that.'

'Sorry if I led him on a bit.'

'No, no, it's best to have the cards on the table. Just to check that you don't have any trumps. It's all going wrong, isn't it? All going wrong for me, all going wrong for Melvyn. It must be costing him a packet.'

'Hmm.' Duffy wouldn't commit himself this early. 'Just out of interest, how did he get involved in the club?'

'I don't know, why does anyone want to do anything as daft as own a football team?'

'Try telling me,' said Duffy.

'Well, sometimes it's in the family. There are a few clubs that are almost like family businesses. Father to son, old aunt Mabel with the casting vote on the Board and so on. Can be very friendly places to work for, big happy family and all that; or they can be bloody awful, with the chairman picking the team. Then there are the people who want to own a club simply because they're football nuts. Love the game, watched it from the terraces, made a pile, and can't wait to have a set of toy footballers to play with, like the toy soldiers they used to have as a kid. They're really keen on the game, come to all the matches, don't bother too much about the bottom line. If things go well, they're probably the best sort to work for.'

'Judging from the way Mr Prosser can't even get the names of his players right, I gather we wouldn't classify him as a football nut?'

Jimmy laughed.

'Well, he does his best, old Melvyn. No, he really tries. He likes saying things like "Class ball" and "Super skills" and "Screamer" – though truth to tell this old team doesn't give him much opportunity to use his vocabulary. No, I think even Melvyn would admit that he's the third sort of owner. Local boy made good, done well for himself, got all he wants, got the big house, the business, the money, and doesn't know what to do with it all of a sudden. Buying the nearest team seems the answer. Nice bit of fame, picture in the paper almost whenever you want it. Local hero and all that. Takes you out of yourself as well – it's a different world, seems glamorous at first, even if it seems a lot less glamorous after a couple of years. And everyone dreams of the Cup run – Wembley, the twin towers, sitting in the Royal Box, all the stuff that never comes.'

'So what does the club need now, if Melvyn Prosser's thinking of pulling out?'

'It needs another nice sucker like Melvyn Prosser,' said Jimmy ruefully.

On the drive to Ealing Duffy suddenly remembered Don Binyon. Stocky, balding, and with an unkind sense of humour, Binyon had been an occasional drinking companion down at the Alligator. Duffy hadn't fucked Binyon – didn't really fancy him – but he'd enjoyed his company. Nice sense of humour, if a bit cutting. Liked to tell people the truth about themselves; very keen on doing that. One evening Duffy, who had been feeling a bit sorry for himself and was punishing the shorts more than he should have done, got a bit talkative. Even tried to explain himself in some funny sort of way. Went on about Carol, and the frame-up, and who he went to bed with. It was a mistake trying to explain himself; not just a mistake, but cheeky as well. Binyon was the guy who explained people. Binyon knew Duffy better than Duffy did.

'Thing about you, Duffy,' said Binyon rather impatiently after his companion had begun to ramble a bit and repeat himself. 'Thing about you, Duffy, is: you're queer. Don't give me any of this bisexual shit. I've heard it all before. It's just a way of saying, Oh no, I'm not really – I'm not really *that*. It's a way of trying to pull back when you're already in it up to your whatsit. You're queer, Duffy. I've seen you operating here often enough to know what you are. You're queer, Duffy. *I'm* queer, *you're* queer, let's have another drink.'

They had another drink.

'But if I'm queer,' said Duffy, who was beginning to feel the strain of the conversation, what with all these shorts, 'if I'm queer, why do I like Carol more than anyone else?'

'Nothing odd about that. Most queers like women. Most women like queers. I'm sure she's a very nice girl, heats a tin of soup up something wonderful. That's got nothing to do with it. And the proof of the pudding, if I may briefly allude to the matter, is the fact that you have a winkle problem with her.'

'But that's because – *that*'s because of that thing that happened ...'

'No, Duffy, the thing that happened just brought it all out into the open. Your winkle problem is your body's way of saying you're queer.'

'But I've been – I've been with girls since,' said Duffy, feeling unaccountably shy all of a sudden.

'How many, eh? How many?' Binyon was almost jeering. Well, not as many as ... but the reason was obvious ... I mean, given that ... Duffy's brain was running out of petrol.

Binyon patted him gently on the shoulder. 'Don't fret yourself, Duffy. And I'm not even trying to get off with you. But you don't fool me, and I don't see why you should fool yourself. If you're not queer, then I'm Selfridges.'

That conversation had worried him. In fact, the next person he'd been to bed with after it had been a girl; but no doubt Binyon would have had an answer for that too. Was he simply gay (Binyon, though gay himself, always preferred the word 'queer', as if he were telling some brutal truth)? In a way, Duffy didn't mind if Binyon was right. He just disliked being regimented like this. You lot stay on this side of the street, and you lot over there keep to that side of the street. No jay-walking; use of the zebra crossing forbidden; and if you try leaping over the pedestrian barrier you'll get run down by a balding man with an unkind sense of humour.

Duffy had remembered this conversation from a couple of years back because of his current preoccupation. Bela Kaposi and his travelling sarcoma. Certificate X. They said you could get AIDS if you were either homosexual or bisexual. Presumably if you were bisexual there was a smaller chance, in basic statistical terms: every girl you'd been to bed with meant one percentage point, or tenth of a percentage point, less chance of night sweats and swollen lymph nodes. On the other hand, there were probably some bisexuals who ended up going to bed with more guys than some homosexuals did. Like himself, for instance. He'd always said that for him the difference between having a girl or a guy was the difference between bacon and egg and bacon and tomato. He still thought that was true. He also had to admit that he'd eaten a lot of breakfast in his time. He looked at the backs of his hands on the driving wheel. Still all clear there, at least. If only he'd known at the time, he could have asked Binyon where your lymph nodes are. It was the sort of thing Binyon would have been sure to know.

Staverton Road, Ealing was a short cul-de-sac of inter-war mock-Tudor semis. Each stretch of pavement supported a pair of lime trees, freshly pollarded. At the end of the street, in front of a decaying brick wall that sealed it off from the railway line, was a car up on blocks; it was shrouded in grey plastic sheeting and its wheels had been removed.

It wasn't hard to spot the headquarters of the Red White and Blue Movement. One of the semis had a flag-pole in its small front garden and was flying the Union Jack. Duffy didn't even bother to check the number he'd been given by the Anti-Nazi League.

The door was answered by a middle-aged man with a red face and small piggy eyes. For someone answering his own front door at eleven o'clock on a Wednesday morning, he was very smartly dressed. He wore the waistcoat and trousers of a dark three-piece suit, a white shirt caught above the elbows by a pair of elasticated metal armlets, a regimental tie, and well-polished black shoes. He also, for some reason, was wearing a bowler hat. Was this Mr Joyce, the organising secretary, answering his front door; or was it perhaps some bailiff on the way out?

'Mr Joyce?'

'Yes.'

'I wanted to ask about the Movement.'

'You press?'

'No.'

'You from the Communists?'

'No.'

'Come in.'

Mr Joyce turned away, hung his bowler on the hat-rack by the front door, and led Duffy into a sunlit kitchen. Duffy had deliberately not overdone the sartorial elegance this morning: denim jacket, denim trousers, lumberjack shirt, heavy boots. He didn't look exactly like one of the Layton Road gang; but he looked fairly tough. He also tuned his voice to a plausible frequency.

Joyce sat him down at the small kitchen table and went off into another room. He returned with a fountain pen and what looked like an application form of some sort. As he took a chair opposite Duffy and gave a perfectly normal smile, he suddenly looked less like a bailiff. More like a doctor about to ask your details. How long have you been homosexual, Mr Duffy? How long have you been bisexual? Would you prefer to be homosexual or bisexual? How long have you had this winkle problem? Maybe I'd better have a look at this winkle for you. No, I think I'd better have a look at this skin discoloration first. Yes, rather as I thought. No point worrying about the winkle problem now. Nurse, fetch me a large bowl of Dettol and the humane killer, would you? Aaaargh.

'And what do you want to ask about the Movement, Mr – er . . . ?'

'Binyon.'

'Mr Binyon.'

'Well, I suppose I want to ask if I can join.' Duffy had decided that he would play things a bit tough, but indicate that he could be respectful if need be to the proper authorities. Like Mr Joyce.

'How did you hear about us?'

'Well, some of the lads on the terraces were talking a bit at half-time. Down at the Athletic on Saturday, down the Layton Road end where I always go; these lads were talking about it at half-time, and I thought, that's the sort of thing for me.'

'May I ask what your politics are, Mr Binyon? First name?'

'Terry. I'm British and proud of it, that's my politics.'

'Yes, well that's a beginning.' Mr Joyce was looking fairly benign, but Duffy couldn't glance up without feeling that the little piggy eyes were examining him very carefully. 'And tell me, what do you think the aims of our Movement are?'

'Beating up the niggers and the Pakis,' said Duffy with a wolfish snigger.

'Oh dear,' said Mr Joyce, laying down his fountain pen, 'we don't seem to have a case of advanced political development here.'

'Nah, it's all right, Mr Joyce, sir, I was just having you on a bit. From what I could gather from the lads and the way they were talking, it's about being a patriot, isn't it?'

'Yes, you could start like that.'

'I mean, I may be out of order here, Mr Joyce, but as far as I understand it, one of the problems with this country is all the politicians are corrupt. Lining their own pockets, going around in big cars, never listening to the people. I mean, if the people want something, then it's their job to give it us, isn't it? I mean, that's what they're there for. Like hanging. Everyone wants hanging, but they won't give it us.'

'I'm with you on that,' said Mr Joyce.

'Or repatriation. Everyone wants that, but they won't give it us.' Duffy tried to remember the handbill he'd been shown by Jimmy Lister. 'I mean, my generation' – Duffy lopped ten to fifteen years off his age, and hoped he could get away with it – 'my generation, it's all, you know, apaffy, that's what it's like. Apaffy. What's the difference between one set of liars and another set of liars? What we need is where the politicians listen to the people and do what they tell them, that's what we need. I mean I want to be proud of being British. I *am* proud of being British,' he added hastily, 'but I'm pissed off with the way this country's been dragged through the mud lately. It is *Great* Britain, isn't it?'

'It is indeed, Mr Binyon. And how are we going to put that Great back into the name of our country?'

Duffy appeared to give the matter some thought.

'Well, I'm only guessing, here. I mean, you must know a lot more about all this than me. But it looks to me that you've got to kick out all the politicians and get in a new set. And it's gotta be Britain for the British. And repatriation. And putting the Great back into Great Britain. And also if they give you too much agg, then it's beating up the niggers and the Pakis.'

This time Mr Joyce allowed himself a conspiratorial chuckle. Duffy felt he wanted a wash.

'But only if they give us, as you put it, too much agg, Mr Binyon.'

'Oh yeah. I mean, fair's fair, isn't it?'

'Fair's fair indeed.'

Mr Joyce unscrewed his fountain pen and began to take Duffy's details. To Binyon's name he added a false address in Paddington and a false age. He confessed to being unemployed. He denied, truthfully, any earlier political affiliation to any other movement. He promised to pay ten pounds annually, or five pounds half-yearly, or three pounds quarterly, and handed over three pounds. He signed where indicated. Then Mr Joyce went away again and returned with two books, one held in each hand: the Bible and Shakespeare. Duffy was asked to stand, and to lay one hand on each book.

'I solemnly swear ...'

I solemnly swear ...'

'That I shall be loyal to Her Majesty the Queen ...'

'That I shall be loyal to Her Majesty the Queen ...'

'And follow the aims and principles of the Red White and Blue Movement ...'

'And follow the aims and – what?'

'Principles.'

'Principles. Aims and principles of the Red White and Blue Movement ...'

'And obey its officers.'

'And obey its officers.'

'Very good. Now we have the medical. Take off your shirt.'

'What?'

'Come on, come on, take off your shirt, just a quick once-over. I am a qualified doctor.'

Duffy reluctantly stripped to the waist.

'Yes, very nice, won't take a minute. No sickle cell anaemia, I hope? Ha ha.'

'Eh?'

'Don't worry, don't worry, no chance of that with *you*.'

Joyce produced an aged stethoscope and applied his attention to Duffy's pectorals. He laid cold fingers on his shoulderblades and tapped. He made Duffy extend his arms full out and checked his fingertips for tremble. Maybe the bloke was a doctor. As well as being a whacko, of course.

'Fine, fine. Don't bother to get dressed again for the moment.'

As Duffy was wondering what came next, Joyce opened his fridge and took out a loaf of sliced white bread. He extracted two pieces and slipped them into the toaster.

'I've had breakfast, Mr Joyce, sir.'

'This isn't breakfast.'

'I think I'd better be off.'

'You've just sworn to obey the officers of the Red White and Blue Movement. Sit down again, Binyon. This won't take long. We've had the medical. Now we're going to have the physical.' Duffy looked at him. Mr Joyce looked at the toaster. '*This*,' he announced, 'is the amusing bit.'

He cleared the few remaining things off the kitchen table and wiped it down with a J cloth. When the toast was done, he lifted the slices out, buttered them thickly, and spread a lot of marmalade on top. He carried them to the table and placed them in the middle, about two feet apart. Then he wiped his hands on the J cloth.

'Arm-wrestling,' he announced. 'Just a little fad of my own. You could call it an initiation ceremony, if you like.'

'Can I put my shirt on?'

'Let's stay as we are, shall we?'

67

Mr Joyce, one steel armlet glinting in the sun, extended his elbow to the middle of the table, white-shirted forearm rising vertically. Duffy, naked to the waist, put forward his own arm.

'Just a moment,' said Mr Joyce, and carefully adjusted the two pieces of toast. Then he repositioned his elbow next to Duffy's; they locked palms and thumbs.

'On a count of three, shall we say? I leave you the count, Mr Binyon.'

Right, you fucking whacko, thought Duffy, and said very quickly, 'One two three.'

Duffy was fit, extremely fit; and the weight training had no doubt strengthened his forearms. But his initial surge made no impact on Mr Joyce, who held the vertical without trouble. Mr Joyce had clearly done this before. So had Duffy, though probably not as often. After the opening surge that failed, Duffy applied steady pressure, but the opposing arm remained immovably vertical. A minute or so of this, and Duffy changed his tactics. He released his pressure, let his arm fall back from midday to one o'clock, and then sharply reapplied the kick. The first two times he did this he got back to the vertical position with no difficulty, but couldn't make any further progress. The third time he tried it, his arm remained stuck at one o'clock. The next time, it was pressed smartly down to two o'clock. The marmalade was only a couple of inches away. Duffy didn't look at Mr Joyce. It was clearly the time for heroics, he decided, for the killer punch. He gathered his strength and surged. Half a second later his forearm was being mashed into the marmalade.

Joyce got up, wiped the palm of his hand on the J cloth, and tossed it to Duffy.

'I didn't want to mess up that nice shirt of yours,' he said.

On their way to the door Joyce explained about the monthly newsletter and about next week's march from Tower Hill. Duffy couldn't get out of the house quickly enough, and gained a yard or so on Mr Joyce in the short corridor leading from the kitchen. He opened the door and turned to say goodbye – or if not goodbye, at least Fuck off. When he turned, he noticed that Mr Joyce was wearing his bowler hat again.

'You know, there are some days when I feel quite normal,' said Duffy.

'Don't let it worry you, love,' replied Carol.

While they were waiting for Duffy's latest culinary creation – frozen pizza from Marks & Spencer – to cook, he told her about his visit to Ealing.

'Lucky he didn't keep his hat on while you were wrestling, Duffy,' she said. 'I don't think you'd have been able to handle it.'

'Do you think I *am* normal?'

'What's normal? There isn't any normal, is there? And if there was, no you wouldn't be normal, course you wouldn't.'

'Oh.' Suddenly, Duffy wanted very much to be normal, even if normal didn't exist.

'But you're not crackers, if that's what you're asking. You're not even odd. Not to me any more. I mean, you probably *are* odd, but I suppose I've got used to it.'

Duffy took the pizzas out of the oven, and put the baking tray to soak before he sat down to eat.

'Very good, Duffy. Delicious. I like the way you've arranged the bits of green pepper.'

Duffy smiled, and accepted the compliment. They often played this game. He liked playing it. For himself, he thought he'd overdone the pizzas. The base was all crispy. Sure, it was *meant* to be crispy, and he'd cooked it for precisely the length of time it said on the box; but it was so crispy that when you cut into it with your knife bits of it went in all directions. Bits of it even went on the floor; and if there was one thing Duffy hated, it was food trodden into the floor. Not that you could exactly tread things *into* a tile floor, but you could certainly squash them on to it, which Duffy didn't like, and you could also pick them up on your shoes and walk them into other rooms, which Duffy liked even less.

'Ever heard of Charlie Magrudo?'

'No. Should I have?'

'No reason. He's apparently some sort of legit villain around here.'

'No. Too far out for West Central to know about him. Unless he was really big.'

'Sure.'

Carol didn't really like hearing about Duffy's jobs. He talked so little about them that when he did she felt she ought to listen, because there was probably something worrying him; but she didn't really like it. It stirred memories. Old memories of when they'd been colleagues at West Central; courting colleagues. And every so often, Duffy would ask her for a bit of help. Help which meant her breaking police regulations. She didn't like that either. She didn't like divided loyalties. She wished he'd got a job which was quite different, which had nothing to do with the Force. She wished he kept a pub – that was what some ex-coppers did. Except that the brewing companies probably weren't looking for publicans whose careers in the Force had ended the way Duffy's had. She hoped he wouldn't ask her for help; if only because she knew she'd probably give in.

'Oh, Duffy, by the way, I found out about lymph nodes.'

'Uh-huh.' Did he really want to know now? Put to the test, he wasn't sure.

'Yes, I asked someone at the station and they said to ask Dr Hawkins.'

'Uh-huh.'

'They're sort of clumps of things. Under your arms and in your neck and in your groin. That's where they are.'

'What are they for?'

'I couldn't really follow it, but they sounded sort of ... useful, from what Dr Hawkins said.'

'Did he say how big they're meant to be?'

'How big? No, I don't think he did. I mean, I think they're pretty small from what he was saying. Do you think you ought to see the doctor?' Carol didn't mention the word cancer, which had come into Dr Hawkins' explanations.

'No.'

'I mean, if you're worrying, I think you ought to see the doctor.' By 'worrying', Carol meant 'worrying more than usual'. If Duffy went to the doctor every time he worried, he might as well rent space in the surgery for a camp bed.

Duffy knew he shouldn't have asked about lymph nodes in the first place. That was always the trouble: you always found out just enough to make things worse, never enough to make things better. Still, at least he knew where these node things were now; that was one step forward. On the other hand, he didn't know how big they were meant to be, so how could he tell if they were swollen? That was one step back. If you could actually feel them, did that mean they were swollen? Or did that mean they were normal, and that if they got any bigger, then they were swollen?

Still, he wasn't going to any doctor, thank you very much. He didn't want them getting out the leper's bell and packing him off to the Welsh mountains.

'No, I'm not worrying, love, I'm fine. Really, I feel fine.'

She looked as if she didn't believe him, so he came round and bent over her and put his arm round her shoulders. He looked at her and smiled, and in a funny sort of way almost felt like kissing her; but they washed up instead. She washed, and he wiped; her wiping was still a bit hit-or-miss, in Duffy's judgment, though her washing was fine. Very thorough.

Carol had an early start the next morning, and by the time Duffy came to bed she was almost asleep. As he climbed in and settled down, he felt something sharp against his leg. He turned on the bedside light again and felt round the sheet a bit. He might have known. He might have known. A small piece of pizza crust. That's *exactly* what he meant. He really would have to give the pizzas five minutes less the next time. There's nothing wrong with soggy crust. People with false teeth must always cook it like that. Unless … unless you didn't kill the bacteria properly if you didn't cook it for the length of time they said on the box. Perhaps Dr Hawkins would know about that. He'd get Carol to ask him. He snuggled up to her back and half-curled round her.

Duffy fell asleep quickly, and the dreams came quickly too. He saw Binyon standing on the bar at the Alligator wearing a black bra and knickers, suspender belt and black stockings. He saw yobbos marching down Layton Road carrying Union Jacks. He saw Binyon and Mr Joyce arm-wrestling. He saw himself keeping goal for the Reliables and every time he went to pick the ball out of the net it had turned into a soggy pizza. He saw Binyon again on the next barstool at the Alligator turning to him and saying, 'The thing about you, Duffy, is that you're a lymph node. You may pretend not to be, but that's what you are.' He saw Melvyn Prosser in his gold Rolls-Royce Corniche reversing over Danny Matson's leg. He saw . . .

He woke up suddenly. He was still curled close to Carol, but two things were different from when he'd gone to sleep. Two things had happened. He was sweating, that was the first thing. He touched his forehead with his fingers and thought, *That*, Duffy, is sweat. *That* is a night sweat.

The second thing which had happened was that he had an erection. He didn't believe this either, but a check with the same fingertips confirmed the fact. *That*, Duffy, he said to himself, is a hard cock. Remember? The first one to come out of hiding for years. With Carol, that is.

There must be some explanation. Perhaps the two surprises were connected. Perhaps his cock was just a lymph node, and it was swollen now because he was going to die in a year or two of this terrible disease. But even so, that was definitely a hard cock.

Thank Christ Carol was asleep.

The next day was one of legwork and small chores. Bits and pieces stuff. He began by dropping round at Danny Matson's digs to invite him down to The Knight Spot that evening. Danny Matson didn't get many invitations, and even a few hours sitting in an old van was better than nothing.

'They found my wallet, by the way. The coppers did.'

'Oh yes? What did they take?'

'Money. Credit card. There wasn't much else. Lucky I didn't have my Trevor Brooking photo in it. They might have taken that.'

'Mmm, they might.' Especially if they'd been Barnsley fans. 'How's the leg?'

'Still there.'

'Keep laughing.'

Then it was back to Layton Road, doing the houses in the opposite order.

At number 57 Mrs Davis answered the door again in her pinafore.

'Oh Wayne,' she called out on seeing Duffy, 'it's that fellow from the *Chronicle* again.' Suddenly she had disappeared and a skinhead in braces took her place. He pushed his face close to Duffy's: either he had bad eyes, or he liked to greet visitors with a head-butt.

'Bugger off, you. You right upset me mam with all that talk of winning the Lucky Numbers.'

'Is your dad in? No, all right, forget it,' Duffy added hurriedly, as the skinhead visibly pondered the need for hostile action.

At number 48 Arthur still wasn't in, and the voice behind the chain gave him even less time than before. At number 37 Mr Bullivant bounced to the door. 'Yes?'

'Mr Bullivant, it's me again.'

'I can see that, laddie.'

'It's just a couple more questions the office wanted me to check out with you.'

'Well, *check them out* then,' said Mr Bullivant, sneering at the phrase.

'Er, how long would you say this trouble's been going on?'

'Since the day they built the ground.'

'But it's got worse in the last – what? three years? one year? three months?'

'Yes.'

'Yes, which, Mr Bullivant?'

'Yes all three.'

'I see. Now, Mr Bullivant, assuming you win your injunction, that might not necessarily be the end of the matter. The club could appeal. How far are you prepared to go with this action?'

'As far as we have to.'

'All the way, you mean.'

'As I said.'

'Mr Bullivant, is the street behind you on this one?'

'No it's right in front of me, silly bugger. Yes of course it is.'

'Have they – had a whip-round for you?'

'Why do you ask?'

'Well, it could cost you a lot of money. If the club fought it all the way.'

'That's our business. Whose side are you on?'

'I'm just trying to find out what's happening. Mr Bullivant, I wondered if perhaps you had a sponsor.'

'How do you mean?'

'Well, is there someone who's sympathetic to what you're doing and who's said he'll cover any expenses you may incur by bringing this action?'

'I wouldn't tell you if there was.'

'Why not?'

'Why should I?'

'Why shouldn't you?'

'Are you what they call a cub reporter?'

'Well, yes, I suppose I am.'

'Thought so. Still haven't written a word in your note-book in two visits. No wonder there's so many lies in the bloody papers. Good day to you.'

Home; and then a call to Ken Marriott. Could Duffy drop by the *Chronicle* to give him the story? Sure. And in exchange, could Ken wangle him into the newspaper's library for ten minutes or so? No problem.

At the *Chronicle* the 'library' turned out to be a false room built into the open-plan office by setting up four walls of filing cabinets from floor to ceiling. Ken found him the file on Charlie Magrudo and left him alone with it.

There were about a dozen items altogether, covering fifteen years. Each had been cut out and glued to a sheet of foolscap paper. Apart from one substantial profile, most of the items were small. LOCAL BUSINESSMAN DONATES SUNSHINE COACH TO VARIETY CLUB and NEW SUPERMARKET TO BE BUILT ON SCHEDULE, PROMISES CONTRACTOR: that sort of thing. From the clippings, Duffy assembled a picture of a hard-working, home-loving, socially aware, charitable, generous and concerned local businessman who was equally loyal to his employees, his family, the Church and the Rotary Club. From time to time other journalists wandered in to use the library. One looked over Duffy's shoulder.

'Charlie Magrudo, eh?'

'Yes.'

'Why are you interested in him?'

'Oh, he's trying to get a contract up in Islington, and

we'd heard he wasn't the cleanest thing that ever drew breath.'

'Charlie Magrudo? Charlie Magrudo's as clean as a whistle. Someone must have been having you on. Pillar of the Rotary Club, and all that.'

'So I'm discovering,' said Duffy. 'Who are you?'

'I'm the chief crime reporter.'

Ken Marriott was quite keen on Duffy's tip-off about the Layton Road residents, and promised he wouldn't let on where the story had come from. Duffy suggested that Ken try to find out if anyone was bankrolling the residents, and added that he had been down there already to ask a few questions; he hoped this didn't affect Ken's chance of getting a good story.

'Don't you worry, old son. I'll get them eating out of my hand. It's surprising how people open up when you tell them you're a journalist.'

'I didn't find that,' said Duffy.

'But you aren't a journalist,' Ken pointed out.

'That's true enough. But you see, I thought the residents mightn't want to talk to me ...'

'Yes?'

'So I said I was you.'

When Duffy got back to his flat there was a message on his answering machine to ring Jimmy Lister. The manager suggested that if Duffy was free he might like to come over to the ground in the next ninety seconds or so.

'Duffy,' said Jimmy as he showed him into his office, 'meet Brendan Domingo.'

'Hi. I hear you're the rising star.'

'Pleased to meet you. Nah, it's all about teamwork really. Get the right set of lads around you and that's what counts.' Brendan looked at the floor. He was large and heavily muscled; though born in Britain, he had very little chance of joining the Red White and Blue Movement. Duffy thought his loyalty to the other players in the Athletic team rather touching. Jimmy Lister had already passed on to Duffy Melvyn Prosser's supportive opinion about his eleven players: this team's a dog, the chairman had said.

'No, if anyone's going to save our necks, it'll be Brendan,' said Jimmy Lister.

'Thanks, Boss,' said Brendan Domingo, still looking at the carpet.

'I gather some of the yobbos are booing you,' said Duffy.

'Yeah. Not very bright of them, is it?' replied Brendan, looking up at Duffy for the first time. Looking up, and then looking down: there was a good seven inches between their heights.

'Does it bother you?'

'Nah,' said Brendan. 'The first time it happened, the very first time, I thought, why don't I just pick up the ball and walk off the pitch? Then I thought, why give them the satisfaction? Second time, I thought, here we go again, and I got rid of the ball a bit quickish. Third time, I thought, no that's what they wanted me to do last time, so I showed them a couple of tricks and hit the post from about twenty-five yards.' Brendan was smiling now, and at ease.

'Tell Duffy what you told me.'

'Well, there's not much to tell really. I was in this pub and there was a geezer there and I think he was trying to fix me.'

'Fix you?'

'Yeah, you know, give me a few hundred quid or

something. Not that we got around to money after I showed him I wasn't interested.'

'Tell me from the beginning. All the details you can remember.'

'Well, like I said, I was in this pub—'

'The Albion,' put in Jimmy Lister.

'—the Albion, right, having a beer and a couple of pies after training, and this fellow comes up. Watched me from the terraces, he says, could he buy me the other half, he says. As I was drinking pints – sorry about that, Boss – I said don't mind if you do. So we started talking about the team, and the results, and this and that, and he finally got around to saying that he had a proposition to put to me. If he hadn't said it was a proposition I probably wouldn't have noticed, he did it really clever.'

'What did he say?'

'Well, he said I was the star of the team, blush, blush, and what would happen if Athletic got relegated, and I said we weren't going to get relegated, we're going to stay up. So he said he liked my attitude, and he said he expected other people would like it too. I ask him what he means, and he says, well look, son, you're under contract, aren't you, two years, three years, five? I tell him three more to go. Well, he says, look at it this way, if Athletic save themselves from relegation, then obviously you're going to carry on in the team, aren't you? Course I am, I say. *But*, he says, suppose some terrible tragedy occurs and you do all go down the toilet, then what's going to happen? The club needs some cash, and the obvious thing to do is to sell their gifted striker. Meaning me. Well, apparently, the word's out on me, he says, people are interested. Nice little Second Division outfit up north, he says. Mid-table, very safe. Couple of years there and I'd

79

be ready for the move into the First Division. So that, he says, is how he sees my career. Choice between another three years slogging along in the basement of the Third Division, or a quick bye-bye and off like a rocket for Brendan. I said I still wasn't getting him, and that's when he said it.'

'What, exactly?' Duffy leaned forward.

'He said that the gentlemen he represented would be more than a bit willing to give a little up front on their investment. On their gifted striker. Meaning me.'

'Very nice,' said Duffy.

'Not very nice is what I thought,' said Brendan.

'No, I meant clever.'

'Yeah, well it wasn't that clever, was it, cause I told him to hop off.'

'Now, Brendan, tell me exactly what this fellow looked like.'

'Oh man, I can't do that. You know, he was sort of average.'

'Old young, big little, well-dressed scruffy?'

'Sort of pretty small; sorry, I mean about your height; oldish – fifty I suppose; thinnish, quite neat, had a mackintosh. But I told him to hop off so he did.'

'How did he talk?'

'Normal. I mean he didn't have a stammer or anything.'

'Colour of his eyes?'

'Man, I don't look at things like that.'

'Hair?'

'Yeah.'

'What do you mean?'

'I mean, like, he had some. He wasn't bald. Look, I'm sorry I don't remember him better. I was eating my pies. And anyway, you know what they say.' He looked up a little mischievously, as if not sure whether to voice his thought. 'All you white folks look the same.'

That evening, Duffy sat in the van with Danny Matson outside The Knight Spot gazing at another collection of white folks who all looked the same. They all looked the same because they all weren't the one person Duffy and Danny were looking for. There were short girls, tall girls, old girls, young girls, girls with cleavage down to their waists and girls as mysteriously shrouded as the car that stood in Mr Joyce's cul-de-sac; but there was no Denise amongst them.

After a couple of hours' waiting, Duffy decided that she might possibly have gone in before they'd arrived. He set off for the entrance to The Knight Spot bearing in his head Danny's less than full description: Denise, dark hair, black dress, showing quite a bit of flesh, dances close to you, hangs around, chases off the other girls, leaves with you, waits while you get the motor, then scarpers. Well, someone was bound to recognise who he was talking about from that, weren't they?

But there was a problem getting into The Knight Spot that evening. The problem was Fat Frankie. Fat Frankie pointed out to Duffy that he wasn't properly dressed for west London's premier club. Fat Frankie pointed out that he wasn't wearing a tie. Fat Frankie said he was the scruffiest bugger who'd tried to get in all evening. When Duffy wanted to remonstrate, Fat Frankie took a lager can and scrunched it up in his great big fist. This impressed Duffy because the lager can was full at the time. What's more, the pressure of Fat Frankie's attentions made the ring-pull burst, and a certain amount of Carling Black Label landed on Duffy's denim jacket. Fat Frankie pointed out that Duffy looked even scruffier now. Duffy wanted to point out to Fat Frankie that he looked like a council rubbish dump; but he took the wiser course of silence.

When he got back to the van, Danny said, 'My leg hurts.'

'Sure,' said Duffy. 'The day's been a dog, anyway. I'll run you home.'

Saturday was match day. Bradford City at home. Duffy rang Jimmy Lister, and apologised for bothering him, but had he had any more thoughts on who might be trying to poach Brendan Domingo, assuming that the attempted bribery had something behind it? Jimmy said he had a short list of three nice little mid-table Second Division outfits up north, and that he'd get on to them first thing on Monday. He knew one of the managers involved, and thought he might get a straight answer.

'But the trouble is, Duffy, when it comes to poaching players, no one obeys the rules. I mean there are decent clubs with decent managers who are still prepared to give a third party a pretty loose budget and turn a blind eye as long as he delivers the goods. We're not talking First Division and six-figure transfers here. We're talking little deals between clubs who are feeling the pinch and can't pay top wages; if some third party persuades a certain player that he'd be happier off with you than where he is, then you wouldn't be human if you didn't thank the party concerned.'

'Yeah, I see that.'

'Coming to the match?'

'Wouldn't miss it.' The first match Athletic had played since Duffy started sharing Jimmy Lister's pay cheque.

'Do you want to see it from the directors' box?' The directors' box was a rectangle of faintly padded seats in the main stand. 'I'll be a bit busy myself. Or I could bung you a ticket at one of the turnstiles.'

'Thanks. No, I'll go down the Layton Road end. I'll give you a wave. No I won't, you'll be able to pick me out easy. I'll be the one cheering Brendan Domingo.'

'Right.'

Duffy made himself a cup of strong coffee before phoning Ken Marriott. 'Maggot, it's Duffy.'

'Duffy? Pull the other one. I'd know that voice anywhere. Isn't it that cub reporter on the *Chronicle*? What's his name, Marriott?'

'Sorry about that. Hope I didn't drop you in it.'

'Nothing I couldn't handle.' Maggot was sounding pleased with himself. 'No, I just went along the street apologising for the extreme ineptitude of the cub we'd foolishly sent along to talk to them. Mr Bullivant was less than impressed by your journalistic skills, I'm afraid, Duffy.'

'Uh-huh.' He'd better let Maggot say his say on this one. It was only fair.

'Said you didn't take a single note. Big fat pad, nice new biro, didn't take a single bloody note.'

'I thought that's the way journalists normally behaved, Maggot.'

'Cheeky. No, Mr Bullivant was very unimpressed. But fortunately I was able to reassure him that your working days at the *Chronicle* were definitely numbered. He said you looked as if you needed a sharp dose of unemployment.'

'Was Mr Bullivant a PT instructor by any chance?'

'Why do you ask?'

'I just thought he looked like one.'

'Duffy, *just thinking* isn't good enough if you're to

continue your brilliant career all the way to the pinnacles of Fleet Street. No, Mr Bullivant is not a PT instructor. He's a retired plasterer who does faith healing and osteopathy in his spare time.'

'How'd you find that out?'

'I asked him, Duffy, I chatted him up and asked him.'

But if Maggot had found out about Mr Bullivant's employment record and skill with stiff joints, he hadn't been able to add much to the small pile of Duffy's knowledge. Number 48 still wouldn't unchain the door; number 57 revealed a rather unforthcoming husband of the pinafored Lucky Numbers player; while Mr Bullivant disclosed no less, and no more, than he'd disclosed to Duffy.

'They could be genuine, you know, Duffy. I mean, I thought they were genuine. Those yobbos can be pretty unsavoury when the fancy takes them.'

'I'm not denying *that*, Maggot, I'm just thinking perhaps there's a Santa Claus somewhere slipping them some advice, and most of all some cash.'

'There's a lot of money in home osteopathy and faith healing. Especially if you don't declare it.'

Perhaps. Duffy didn't think that was the answer. And besides, would number 57 think of suing the club over the yobbos when the son of the house turned out to be a prize yobbo himself?

At opening time Duffy went to the Albion and bought the barman a drink. Sure, he worked here every lunchtime. Yes, and yesterday lunchtime. Littlish fellow, fiftyish, neat, mackintosh? No, don't remember him. He wouldn't have been a regular. How do you know? Well, the regulars are the ones I remember, and the ones I don't remember aren't regular. Simple. Anyway, Duffy went on, this bloke in the mac was with Brendan Domingo.

84

Who? Brendan Domingo, big fellow, very muscular, dark skin. Oh, you mean, coloured fellow? Yes, that's Brendan Domingo. Oh that's *Brendan Domingo*, is it? No, don't remember him, he can't be a regular. Who *is* Brendan Domingo anyway? Tell you this for nothing, all these coloured chaps look alike to me. Cheers!

Rather than face the Albion's lukewarm meat pies, Duffy went home for a slimmer's lunch. There'd been a lot more brown bread and yoghurt around Duffy's kitchen lately. Duffy was worried about getting fat. Duffy was also worried about not having enough to eat and losing his strength. So he had the brown bread and the yoghurt for stopping getting fat; and he had some streaky bacon, cheese and a bottle of Guinness for making him not lose his strength. That was about the right balance. After lunch he felt his neck and his armpits; then undid his trousers and dabbled in his groin. The trouble was, there seemed to be little lumps everywhere. Maybe his lymph nodes were really getting out of hand. Maybe he only had a couple of hours to live. That night sweat he'd had felt a real killer. It had even, as he recalled, given him hallucinations about other parts of his body.

By a bit of lawyer's know-how, the club had managed to delay its courtroom confrontation with the Layton Road residents for a few days. Even so, this might be the last time the yobbos would stomp down the street, Duffy thought, as he joined the crowd. There seemed to be quite a few policemen around; a couple even standing right outside Mr Bullivant's house. Perhaps the club had made a few suggestions to the coppers, and a special ablutions watch was being kept on number 37.

Just inside the ground the coppers were searching everyone who was young, male and not obviously in a wheelchair. Anyone wearing big boots was taken aside and had his toes introduced to a constable's heel. Just checking for steel toecaps. Sir. The police took away everything that could be thrown, everything that could be drunk, and everything that could be used for sticking into someone else. No metal combs, no beer cans, full or empty; no, you won't be needing that set of darts this afternoon, lad, come and collect it afterwards. A mound of potentially lethal junk was piled behind the police lines. Lots of stuff got smuggled in all the same – that was why they had a WPC searching the occasional tough girl who dared to stand at the Layton Road end – but at least this caught some of the heavier ammunition. If the coppers didn't search every single yobbo every single time, they'd be bringing in Armalites and assembling do-it-yourself bazooka kits on the terraces before you knew where you were.

Past the police lines and the ground began to display its smells and sounds and sights. A hamburger stall stood near the entrance to the toilets: the two smells not cancelling one another but mixing together into a richer, denser brew. The screechy public address system churned out pop records which the club secretary – who preferred Herb Alpert and the Tijuana Brass himself – imagined that the better class of customer wished to hear. Programme sellers in booths labelled PROGRAMMES bellowed 'PROGRAMMES!', to help anyone partially sighted who might be in the vicinity. Fans rushed past as if their favourite place on the terracing was about to be stolen, even though the ground held fifteen thousand and the expected attendance was two and a half. A man dressed in the club's blue-and-white waved a board of rosettes and badges, but was meeting some dogged consumer resistance.

A light drizzle was beginning to fall as Duffy made his way up the couple of dozen concrete steps leading to the terraces. The Layton Road end was also known as the Piggeries end, for some forgotten historical reason; though in recent years the nickname had become appropriate again with the arrival of the yobbos. From time to time they would acknowledge the fact with a jolly chant of 'ATH-LE-TIC-OINK-OINK-OINK.'

Up on the terraces, away from the smells and the programme sellers, even a run-down little ground like this had its charm. There it was, all laid out: the bright pitch, the fresh markings, the nice rectangular goals. Apart from a few advertisement hoardings, you couldn't see anything that wasn't to do with the game. Just the pitch, the terraces, the fans; beyond, only the sky and the floodlights rearing up at the four corners of the ground. Duffy felt excited.

He took a position halfway up the Piggeries terrace and a bit to the left, where he could watch both the game and the yobbos without too much trouble. The exchange of pleasantries between the Athletic fans at this end and the Bradford fans at the other had already begun. 'ATH-LE-TIC' – 'SHIT' – 'ATH-LE-TIC'- 'SHIT' – 'ATH-LE-TIC'- 'SHIT'. And then, a bit later, the welcoming reply: 'CIIIII-TY' – 'SHIT' – 'CIIIII-TY' – 'SHIT' – 'CIIIII-TY' – 'SHIT'.

After a while, both sets of fans began to tire of this. The City supporters, whose club occupied a safe position in the top ten of the Division, decided to predict Athletic's fate come the end of the season, 'GOING DOWN GOING DOWN GOING DOWN,' they chanted, 'GOING DOWN GOING DOWN GOING DOW-OW-N.' The Layton Roaders couldn't think up any immediate riposte, but after a while they sketched a lively self-portrait for the City fans. 'WE ARE THE ANIMALS — OINK OINK OINK. WE ARE THE ANIMALS — OINK OINK OINK. WE ARE ...' and so on until the two sides trotted out. The public address cheerfully cut off Cilla Black in mid-phrase and began running through the teams. Each Athletic name was dutifully cheered by the home fans and booed by the away fans; all except that of Brendan Domingo, which was booed by both sets of fans. Duffy noticed that Brendan didn't even pause in his warm-up. He carried on nonchalantly laying the ball off to a chunky midfielder, sprinting a few yards and taking a return pass. I'd move on, mate, if I were you, thought Duffy. Nice little Second Division outfit somewhere. They might even have another black player in the side. Not that you probably need the company; it just makes it harder for the animals when they find they're booing almost one-fifth of their own side. Duffy had two solutions for Brendan and Jimmy Lister and Melvyn Prosser. One: sell Brendan, make the club a few bob, advance the player's career and get him into a less unsavoury outfit (though this, he recalled, was exactly what someone seemed to be trying to do already). Two: keep Brendan, sell the other ten players, and buy ten new black players. That would sort the Piggeries end out; it might be just a bit too much for their poor brains to handle.

The match was one of those uneven, end-of-season bouts between differently motivated sides. Athletic needed to win if they were to have any chance of lifting themselves out of the bottom three in the table; City didn't need the points, and were already turning their thoughts to next season. This ought to have given the advantage to Athletic, but it didn't: they were fretful, wound-up, over-eager; they pressed too hard and left themselves open at the back; two players would often go for the same ball in their keenness to do something, anything. City, on the other hand, with only their win bonus to worry about, were more relaxed; they tried a few little tricks, but didn't worry if they failed to come off. One side was jumpy and frantic; the other ambitious but lethargic. The midfield became clogged, and for all Athletic's anxious bustle they never troubled the City goalkeeper. The most effective piece of action in the first half came from the coppers: perhaps they were as bored as most of the spectators. On a given signal, twenty of them suddenly sprinted up the Layton Road terrace, burst their way into the phalanx of yobbos, made a path to its centre and stood there, four deep and five across, watching the game and chatting up the yobbos. Duffy laughed a bit at this. It was obviously a new tactic since his days in the Force. Just standing there, in the middle of the boot-boys, watching the game and gassing away. Not trying to be nice to the yobbos – that wasn't the point; just embarrassing the hell out of them for ten minutes or so. Then the coppers eased themselves away and went to look elsewhere.

The first half was what Melvyn Prosser would have called a bow-wow. City were clearly the more skilful side, but weren't too bothered either way; Athletic didn't seem to have any ideas about attacking except to win throw-ins and occasional corners, tactics which City had clearly seen before. At half-time, as Cilla Black took up her song from the beginning again, Duffy moved across to the fringe of the yobbos. They looked young to Duffy: very young, very unhealthy, and very tough. He saw lots of grey skins and pimples and unformed faces; yet he bet most of them would run Mr Joyce closer at arm-wrestling than he had done. None of them wore a rosette, or a badge, or anything indicating support for Athletic. Hair: short. Height: normal. Special characteristics: zero consumption of yoghurt and health foods.

Duffy picked out a largish youth wearing a Union Jack T-shirt and sidled up to him. He decided not to start by praising the skills of Brendan Domingo.

'Playing rubbish, aren't they?' he said casually.

Union Jack didn't reply.

'You wiv … the Movement?' he tried next. This got a reply.

'You what?'

'You wiv the Red White and Blue? You going down Tower Hill next week?' A couple of those nearby were now listening to the exchange.

'Haven't seen you down this end before.'

'Name's Des.' He was getting through a lot of names this week, he thought.

Union Jack, Duffy noticed, had a gold stud in his left ear. But there seemed little chance that he was a regular at the Alligator.

'Haven't seen you down this end before.'

'You going down Tower Hill next week?'

There was a long pause. Three of the yobbos on the step below had turned round and were staring at Duffy. Union Jack was ignoring him, and gazing down at the pitch. Finally he found something to say.

'I don't fink it's good for your elf, standing ere.'

Duffy retreated.

The Layton Roaders seemed to enjoy the second half more. Waddington, City's tubby left-back, tried a long-range shot and nearly hit the corner flag. 'ooooooh,

WANKY-WANKY, WANKY-WANKY-WANKY-WANKY WA-DDING-TON; OOH, WANKY-WANKY, WANKY-WANKY-WANKY-WANKY WA-DDING-TON.' The referee failed to give a penalty when an Athletic midfielder tripped over his own feet in sheer excitement at getting in the opposing area. 'KILL THE REFEREE, KILL THE REF-EREE, EE-AI-ADDIO, KILL THE REFEREE.' Brendan Domingo took a lofted ball from the wing, killed it on the inside of his knee, let it roll down his calf, and laid it off swiftly to give Danny Matson's replacement a scoring chance. 'BRENDAN IS A FAIRY, BRENDAN IS A FAIRY, BRENDAN IS A FAIRY.'

With ten minutes to go, and the City fans setting up another chant of 'GOING DOWN GOING DOWN GOING DOWN', Athletic fiddled a corner. Short to the near post, headed on, headed out, turned back, miskicked, headed back in, not cleared, twenty-one different players to choose from, and Brendan, off-balance, toe-poked it home from about five yards out. The City fans were silent; the Layton Roaders were silent; Duffy, despite his promise to Jimmy Lister, decided not to draw attention to himself; there were a few claps and squeaks from the main stand, re-peated at about the same volume when the public address announced the scorer's name. Move on, Duffy whispered to Domingo, move on; this lot don't deserve you.

Ten minutes later, Athletic had gained victory and three points; when news of the other matches came through, it was confirmed that they were out of the bottom three. They were still in the bottom four, but looking at the points won and the games to play, it meant that at least the future was in the side's own hands. If they got the results, they'd stay up, no matter what the other teams did.

Jimmy Lister was still smiling when Duffy wandered into his office.

'Good result,' said Duffy.

'The lads did the business. They did the business. What more can you ask?'

Danny Matson, who could handle coming to the games if not going to The Knight Spot, was sitting in a chair by the Boss's desk and smiling too.

'Big Bren came good just when we needed him.'

Big Bren and ten other damp-haired players had the biggest smiles of all.

'Hey, Boss,' Brendan shouted across the room, 'I hope you saw how I planned the whole movement.' Everyone laughed.

'I'm proud of you, lads,' said Jimmy Lister. 'Never stopped battling. Full ninety minutes. Real team effort. Proud of every one of you.' And he went round the room slapping the players and punching them playfully.

'Hey, Boss, OK if I have a few beers tonight?' shouted Brendan.

'You can have as many halves as you like,' said the Boss.

Brendan had quite a lot of halves that evening. Duffy had a tomato juice followed by a low-alcohol lager. Well, he'd never been a Saturday-night raver; or at least, not Saturday night rather than any other night. What about Carol, though, he wondered, as he divided their boil-in-a-bag cod dinner into two portions. Maybe she wanted to be taken out on a Saturday night?

Later, as Carol was falling asleep and Duffy lay tucked up with her, he got another erection. He held his breath. She stirred slightly, and moved her bottom a little.

'Duffy,' she murmured, 'is there anyone else in this bed apart from the two of us?'

'Not that I know of,' he answered. He was feeling – almost hearing – a slow, fat, deadly drop of sweat begin to trickle down his temple.

'Then I must be dreaming,' she said, and slipped off into sleep.

Brendan Domingo, despite the opinion of the Layton Road yobbos, was not a fairy. Brendan Domingo, like Duffy, had an erection. Whether this was a good idea or not, he wasn't to know at the time.

Half-time

'Shhh,' went Geoff Bell; and the whole team obeyed.

Bell was not one of the Reliables' star players. He was heavy in the leg, didn't train enough, and secretly preferred rugby. He also wore glasses, but left them in the dressing room, which was a handicap; he'd tried contact lenses, but they irritated his eyes a lot, and he was afraid of losing one on the pitch. They used to tell him that if he could get used to lenses he might develop into a player with vision, like Maggot; but they didn't really mean it.

Geoff Bell usually occupied a loose, freeish position in midfield. It was free because however many instructions you gave him, he never managed to follow them. It was a mystery why he ever wanted to play the game. It was a mystery to opponents why the Reliables ever bothered to pick him; but then opponents never saw the Reliables more than once a season, and they normally assumed Bell was a last-minute substitute. Bell was never a last-minute substitute. If it was a home game, his was the first name to be pencilled in; if it was an away game, his was the first to be left out.

Home matches were always played at the recreation ground, and the Reliables, partly by being so reliable, were routinely allotted pitch A, alongside their own small changing hut. There were two tiny rooms, three showers and a toilet. According to a long-established and friendly ritual, the two sides would retire to the hut at half-time, where the away side would find in its room a small tray bearing six halved oranges, a packet of chocolate wholemeal, four pints of milk and half a bottle of whisky. At first some of the teams were suspicious about the whisky, but most of them worked out that half a bottle between eleven wasn't going to make anybody's game woozy; it was simply a nice gesture, and it made teams look forward to playing the Reliables at the recreation ground.

Partly it was a nice gesture; but it also ensured that opponents didn't decide that the macho thing to do at half-time was stay out on the pitch and get in some shooting practice.

Geoff Bell was crouched on a bench with his hands pressed tight to his ears. Anyone would have thought he was sunk in gloom at the memory of his first-half performance. Anyone who thought that would have been wrong. For seven of the fifteen minutes that half-time occupied, the home dressing room was entirely silent. Then Geoff Bell sat up, took out an earphone and said, 'Right. Got it.'

The other ten waited attentively. This was Bell's moment of importance, and he played it for all it was worth; he was dry, authoritative and irrebuttable.

'Right. For a start they know they've got the skinning of our right-back. Sorry about that, Tommo; the winger says he's got you on toast. Second, they think that someone called Phil, who I think must be that ginge, has got the complete run of the midfield, but they want him to push a lot further forward in the second half. They say it's all very well walking over the midfield but it's no good unless it puts you in business on the edge of the penalty area. They're not very impressed by my play; in fact I think I caught the phrase "complete wanker" at one point.'

The other ten laughed. This was just like Geoff. He could easily have edited that bit out, but he seemed to have some curious determination to tell everything that went on. This made them not mind so much when he didn't tone down some of the comments about the rest of them.

'Maggot, there was also a bit about you.'

'Oh yes?' said Ken Marriott hopefully.

'Yes, they say they think you're a psycho.'

'Oh. Didn't they say anything about my vision?'

'Just that you're a psycho and that the first three times you get the ball in the second half they're going to give you a whacking.'

'Oh dear.'

'They think that only Barney – at least, I think that's who they must mean by the bald smarmy one – sorry about that, Barney – is any threat to the defence. They say he's a bit slow but turns nicely for a fat man, and might have pinched one right on the whistle if they hadn't closed him down in time.'

Barney smiled. He didn't mind being called fat and smarmy in the least as long as they had picked him out as the most subtle and venomous operator amongst the Reliables.

'Anything about me?' said Duffy.

'They said they think you're a terrific keeper, very fast, very brave, reflexes like a cat and a lovely pair of hands. The only thing stopping them giving us a real hiding.'

Duffy grinned to himself with quiet pleasure; until he noticed that all the others were grinning with very noisy pleasure.

'Sorry, Duffy, nothing at all.'

'Oh, well.'

'They're pretty confident they've got the beating of us, but they're going to play it fairly quiet for the first ten minutes or so, apart from stomping on our psycho, that is, and then push a couple more men forward for quarter of an hour to see if they can nick another goal, and then whatever happens they'll pull them both back again. One will be wide on the right, the other one I think is the big centre-back who's going to be allowed to come forward whenever he feels like it. That's about all. Oh, and they said that someone they call the young lad – I guess that must be you, Karl – looks quite sharp, but they think he's a bit out of his depth at this level of the game.'

'Fucking hell,' said Karl French. 'They're only a pub-load of wankers.'

'Just passing on what the man said.'

'Which one said that,' asked Karl, 'which one? I'll bloody do him, second half.'

'Just voices, voices,' said Bell.

'Quite,' said Micky Baker, captain and left-back of the Reliables. 'For a start, you won't do anyone, Karl. That's not the point of the whole thing. That just undoes everything. Now, quickly, lads, we've only got a couple of minutes, so concentrate.'

Barney checked that the door was quite shut, and Micky gave his instructions.

'First, we'll swap our full-backs over. I was thinking I'd have to take that winger of theirs anyway. OK, Tommo? I'll follow him, and if he switches wings, we switch. You take my chap, he's a bit less tricky. Always tries to go on the outside, too; I think he's only got one foot. Next, we don't give Karl the ball for ten minutes.'

'Come off it,' said Karl.

'No, I'm serious. You didn't get much of a sniff in the first half, so they don't know what you can do. We know what you can do. So for the first ten minutes while they're keeping it tight, we keep it tight, and any ball that comes to you, you get rid of fairly quickly. Then, when they push the extra men forward and are only watching out for Barney, who they think is a bit slow anyway, we try to get the two of you forward quickly on the break. Anyone gets the ball midfield, look up and try and spot Karl, whip it up to him quickly and let him run at them. Give them the shock of their lives if he does the business on them.'

Karl grinned. 'I like it.'

'Now, what else?'

'What else?' said Maggot. 'What else? They're going to beat me up, that's what else.'

'No they're not,' said Micky soothingly. 'We can't stop them trying – I mean, not without letting on that we've been eavesdropping – but we can give them a bit of their own back. Every time they have a dig at you, we clobber the ginge.'

'That won't make *me* feel better,' complained Maggot.

'No, but it'll stop the ginge, which has to be priority number one.'

'You're a hard man, skipper.'

'Come off it, Maggot, we won't let them do anything too bad to you.'

'They want to destroy my vision,' said Maggot mournfully.

'Shut up, Maggot,' most of the team counselled. Micky Baker unscrewed the cap of the home team's half-bottle of whisky and, as was the custom, offered the first gulp to Bell. 'Nice work, Geoff.'

Duffy grinned across at Bell. It had been Duffy who'd first suggested him for a place in the Reliables. Geoff was a sort of friend, though more of a business associate – someone to run to for advice on the technical side of things. Geoff Bell was good with machines, and cameras, and recorders, and electricity, and all the things that Duffy was bad with. His expertise, however, wasn't quite so great when it came to estimating the distance that a spheroid object of known weight would travel when struck by his own boot; and for the first couple of games Duffy had watched with some embarrassment as terrible things kept happening in the vicinity of Geoff Bell.

'Still struggling with his form, is he?' asked Micky Baker after Bell's fourth game.

'Well, you know how hard it is coming into a strange team playing a different system,' Duffy replied defensively.

'Yeah, I suppose it must seem like a strange system to him – kicking the ball along the ground to someone on your own side and then trying to get it into the opposite net.'

Even Duffy had thought Bell lucky to get a fifth outing with the Reliables. On that occasion they were four–nil down at half-time and Bell sat with his head in his hands, apparently absorbing the various reproaches that were flying around. In fact, he was listening on an earphone to the small bug he'd placed in the visiting team's dressing room. Suddenly he upped and told them the whole of the opposition's plans – and their predicted result of eight–nil.

At first the Reliables hadn't known how to react; but given that they were four–nil down and carrying this joker in midfield, they decided that the only thing they could do was treat it all as a giggle. So they had a good laugh, and then they thought, Well, if this mad passenger of ours really has found out this stuff for us we may as well try using it. They went out for the second half in rather a humorous frame of mind, and they came back in rather a serious frame of mind, having reduced the deficit to four–two and come very close to squeezing a third goal. Then they sat down and had a think, and decided that since other sides were always doing things which weren't quite in the spirit of the game – like including the odd cowboy to inject a bit of class – why shouldn't the Reliables have their own little way of doing things? It wasn't as if they were breaking rules on the pitch, or bribing the ref. A few of them felt uneasy about it at first, but they soon got used to it; and the fact that they didn't play Bell away from home (where you normally just stood shivering on the pitch at half-time) made it all seem more acceptable. It became a jolly part of the home-game ritual, along with the oranges, the milk and the whisky.

As they walked out again, one–nil down against the pub side and expecting a certain amount of agg, Geoff Bell caught up with Duffy.

'I'm afraid they did say something about you.'

'Oh yeah?'

'Only as it wasn't of direct tactical relevance I didn't pass it on in front of the others.'

'Oh yeah?'

'They said you were rather small for a goalkeeper.'

'Thanks, Geoff. Thanks a mil.'

Second Half

'Good three points.'

Brendan looked up.

'Oh. Yeah. Thanks.'

Brendan was sitting by himself in a corner seat of the Albion saloon bar. It was a Saturday night, and the pub was at its fullest; a noisy game of darts was whooping away in one corner, and the evening's serious drunks were beginning to feel a bit combative. The more the noise rose, the more people had to shout, and the more the noise rose. Saturday night's husbands were squeezing another pint into their elasticated stomachs before toddling home for the weekly legover. Saturday night's smokers had bought themselves a cigar for a change, just to make the air thicker. Saturday night's solitary drinkers felt the more solitary as those around them rowdily demonstrated that, whatever else they might lack in their lives, they certainly didn't lack friends.

All except Brendan. To Brendan the Albion seemed almost quiet, and he didn't mind in the least being alone. Perhaps this was because he'd come on from Benny's after leaving the other lads to it. Benny's was where some of the team went when The Knight Spot began to feel a bit of a chore, a bit like another public appearance. Benny's was small, deafening and cheap; while the girls, as Athletic's keeper had once enthusiastically explained to Brendan, were very, very slaggy. Brendan used to go along, simply because being with the lads helped him come down after a match; and then, an hour or two later, he'd plead early bedtime, and the lads would say, Hey, we know you, Brendan, you just don't like our girls, you're popping down The Palm Tree for a bit of your own, aren't you, let's all go down there, lads, big Bren'll get us in; and he'd smile and say, No, really, it's early bedtime, and then paying them back a bit he'd say, Anyway I wouldn't take you down The Palm Tree, you guys ain't *classy* enough to mix with the chicks down there, and they'd all roar and slap him about a bit and shout Good old Bren, and then he'd slip away for a couple of quiet halves down at the Albion.

'Mind you, it wasn't exactly a great spectacle, if you don't mind my saying so.'

Brendan laughed.

'And I wouldn't mind betting you didn't know where you were putting it when you scored.'

Brendan laughed again.

'Well, I knew it wasn't going to be an own goal.'

'Can I buy the conquering hero a drink?'

'Pleasure.'

'Bacardi and coke?' she suggested. Was she teasing?

'Half of best, thanks.'

'Half of best it is.'

She was called Maggie, she said, and she dressed in black. Shoes, tights, shortish skirt that was almost a ra-ra but not quite, turtleneck sweater. Probably she did it because she had lots of blonde hair; Brendan had to admit that the contrast was striking. Footballers are meant to prefer blondes, he knew that. It wasn't so much true nowadays, but there was a time in the sixties and early seventies when every footballer wanted a blonde wife to go with the Jag and the ranch-style house out Chingford way. They used to say that you could tell if a footballer was First Division or not by looking at the roots of his wife's hair. If you saw little black quarters of an inch you knew the fellow was Second Division. If you could see from across the room that the wife had been doing it herself with peroxide, then he was probably Third or Fourth. There was an awful lot of dyeing in those days: some of the supporters' clubs could have opened a ladies' hairdressing business on the side.

Maggie knew a bit about football. Not a lot, she admitted; she'd only really got keen on the game this season, but she came to all the home matches. She was a good listener, and she didn't ask stupid questions. That was the trouble with fans, Brendan had to admit to himself. At first he'd thought all fans were a good thing – anyone who liked the game was a good thing, and anyone who thought Brendan was a great player was an even better thing; but after a while you could get enough of the fans. Or at least, you could get enough of two kinds of fans. The first lot were the know-nothings, who giggled and nudged one another and wondered if that wasn't big Brendan Domingo over there and mustn't it be smashing to be a professional footballer and wasn't that a screamer of a goal you scored against Port Vale, when it had only gone in because it had bounced off your knee and the keeper had been out of position and fretting about his mortgage repayments. The second lot were the know-alls, who'd seen Stanley Matthews years before you were born, lad, who could tell you exactly what was wrong with the club, the management, and most of all with you and your play – too deep or too far forward, too wide or too central, holding the ball too long or getting rid of it too quickly. Sometimes Brendan thought that these two kinds of fans were the only ones who ever came to the matches. Football was, in a way, simpler than either of them imagined. You practised a lot, and you went out there and did your best, your very best, every week; it was a job, but a job that you liked; and though you were pretty good at it, there were lots of other people who were better. That was how Brendan saw the game.

'Does it get to you when they boo you?'

'No. Yes. Well, not at the time, because you're concentrating, and you don't want to give them any satisfaction. But afterwards, I suppose, yeah, it does get you down a bit.'

'Why do they do it?'

'I think they don't like my blond hair and big blue eyes,' said Brendan.

That seemed to relax them a bit. It was as if he'd said, You see, one of the things about me is, I'm black; you may not have noticed, but I thought I ought to point it out to you. And when she'd joined in his laugh, it had meant, Funny you should say that thing about being black; I thought there was something about you, but I just couldn't put my finger on it.

Brendan stood up.

'Can I get you a small gin with a half-bottle of tonic, twist of lemon and plenty of ice?' It was his tease back.

'Drambuie and lemonade,' she said, and they both laughed. He much preferred the Albion to Benny's. And truth to tell, he wasn't all that keen on The Palm Tree.

They stayed until nearly closing time, and Brendan thought, I could go for you. Problems, of course; but I could go for you.

'Do you feel all drained after a match?'

'Depends. If you lose, you do. Just want to put your head in a bucket. Wish you didn't have to get through Sunday before you can go back to the ground and start working on things. If you win you just feel, give me half an hour, and I'll go out and play another game. You feel kind of set up. I dunno.'

'Well, I'm glad you won today.'

'So am I. Those three points are gold dust.'

She lived just off Twyford Avenue; would he drop her? Sure, of course, he said, noting that she said drop rather than run home or see home, or any of those other phrases that you listen out for very carefully. But as he put the handbrake on and left the engine running, she said, 'I haven't any coffee, but I've got some Drambuie and lemonade in the fridge.'

'When in Rome,' said Brendan with a laugh.

They sat in the kitchen and had a few more drinks than they ought to have done; there wasn't any doubt about that. Maggie was mixing them, and it seemed to Brendan that each one was a little stronger than the last. When on about the fourth, he said, 'Hey, is there any lemonade in this one?'

She came over to his chair, sat herself down on his knee, stroked her hand against his cheek and said, 'Is this the big centre-forward calling for more lemonade?'

Brendan thought, I'm not exactly a *centre-forward*, you don't use words like that. He felt it highly important to pass on this piece of information.

'I'm not exactly a centre-forward,' he said very seriously, 'It's more that I play up front. I'm a target man.'

'Oh, you're a target man, are you? Well, all I can say is, Bull's-eye!'

Brendan laughed, and felt uneasy at the same time. This was the awkward bit; this was the bit he'd have to leave up to her. True, she was sitting on his lap, but something always held him back a bit with white girls. Sure, he was meant to be all relaxed and sexy and macho, and limbo-dance under her bed or whatever; but it wasn't like that when it came down to it. He hadn't even put his hand on her leg yet, even though her leg was very close to his hand, and her skirt was almost a ra-ra. That Drambuie definitely did need some more lemonade in it. The thing was, of course, he really did rather like her.

'It's all right,' she said, leaning into him until her head was on his shoulder and her mouth not far from his ear. 'It's all right. It's only called going to bed.'

He chuckled.

'Oh, is that what it's called? I thought only the grown-ups did that.'

She got off his lap, pulled him out of the kitchen, pushed him into the bedroom and disappeared, shutting the door behind her. For a moment he wasn't entirely sure what was happening – perhaps she'd gone off to sleep on the couch? – but at any rate, here was a bedroom, here was a bed, and here he was expected to sleep. So he undressed, climbed into bed, smelt the sheets, and thought, It's been a good day, Brendan, say what you will, three points plus a nice girl has got to be better than relegation and a wank, hasn't it? He wasn't quite sure what to do about the overhead light. He'd left it on when he got into bed. Should he get out, turn it off and put the bedside lamp on instead? He didn't yet know whether or not he was going to get company. He supposed the lads were still booz-ing down at Benny's. He hoped Danny Matson wasn't waiting up for him at their digs. He liked Danny, but they'd somehow seen less of one another since Danny's leg went. He'd better make more of an effort for Danny. Must be awful. Maybe Maggie's got a friend who likes footballers with their legs in plaster?

There was a distant noise of water running through pipes, then a door was shut, then another door was opened. This door, thought Brendan, who had an arm across his eyes to shield them from the overhead light. Then the light went off and the door was closed. He felt a pull on the sheets and a press of flesh and a knee hit him in the thigh and he apologised, even though it wasn't his fault.

'Do you remember, in the pub,' she said.

'What's that?'

'We were talking about the match and I said I thought you didn't know where you were putting it when you scored.'

'Yeah.'

'Well, I hope you do now,' she said, and pressed even closer.

'You dirty girl,' he said, pushing her on to her back and kissing her for the first time, and not very accurately, given that the light was off. 'You dirty girl. Have to wash your mouth out with soap.'

'Or something,' she said. As she reached down and grabbed his cock, he heard a faint chant in the back of his head. 'Brendan is a fairy, Brendan is a fairy.' If the Layton Road enders were interested, then Maggie was holding Exhibit A.

Yes, that was a good feeling, Brendan thought, as she eased him inside her. That was a good feeling. The good feelings went on, for a bit, at least. Then Brendan thought Ow. The good feelings returned, until Brendan thought

Ow again but laughed a bit, because it was only her nails in his ribs, and that was all part of the game. The next time it happened it was much harder, and he said, 'Ow, that hurts, you know.'

She didn't reply. It was dark; the curtains were thick; she had given up saying things to him that were a bit dirty; they were just there, in the dark, silent, fucking. Lots closer, and yet a bit more distant, Brendan thought; but he didn't think much, and they carried on fucking.

They started getting a bit noisier. She scratched at his ribs a bit more and he whispered, 'Maggie,' but she didn't seem to be hearing him. She reached up and got hold of his ears and seemed to be telling him what to do by pulling on them; and that seemed to be nice too, until suddenly she reached round the back of his neck and pulled his head down very hard and there was a cracking sound as his forehead hit her nose and he felt as if he'd gone for a fifty-fifty ball and a defender had booted him in the face, but still she didn't say anything or make a sound. Brendan felt uneasy, but there didn't seem to be any point in not carrying on. Christ his head hurt. Why ever had she done that? He wouldn't let her get hold of his ears again.

She didn't get hold of his ears again. She reached up and dug both her hands into his cheeks and dragged both sets of nails across his face and howled while she did this. She was attacking him and howling, and Brendan found it definitely a bit scary but also, somewhere, he had to admit, a bit exciting. She reached for his face with her nails again and he pushed her hands away and said 'No,' and she reached again and he stopped her and she suddenly got noisier and reached again and howled and he thought Christ she's hysterical and the next time she reached he hit her across the face, and she said, 'Fuck me, hit me,' and after she went for him again it didn't seem such a bad idea, and especially when he felt blood on his face and she was really going at him with her nails and he hit her again and she shouted, 'Fuck me, hit me, fuck me, hit me,' and everything seemed to get noisier and more painful and more exciting because that was what she was telling him to do, and with a lot of bellowing he came inside her and then she suddenly stopped. Just stopped everything. She lay completely still and said nothing, and it was utterly dark and he wondered if she was having a fit or had passed out or needed a glass of water or something, and he rolled off her and whispered, 'Maggie?'

She reached across with an arm and patted him on the nearest bit she could find, as if to say, 'It's all right, I'm all right,' and after a while he felt the bed shift and heard the door open and close. A minute or two passed, and he waited for the sound of water running through pipes, but it didn't come. What he heard instead was the slam of a door, so loud that it shook the walls of the flat, and then, close at hand, too close, much too close, the sound of someone screaming. Brendan thought that maybe things weren't all right after all. When he switched on the bedside light and saw the blood on the pillow, and the blood on his hand, and looked in the mirror and saw the blood on his face, he knew that things weren't all right in any way. He ran for his clothes, and started putting them on in a panic, and they were all in the wrong order, and none of them seemed to fit – Hey, why am I getting into someone else's clothes? – but he struggled and tugged and finally made it, and ran for the front door and slammed it, not caring, and got to his car. As he turned the ignition key he knew, without the least doubt, that things weren't ever, ever going to be all right again.

The detective-sergeant thought it strange that he was calling at the same set of digs for the second time this month. Bloody footballers. Bloody football. Horrible game, played by thugs, watched by yobs. Cricket was the detective-sergeant's game. When was the last time you heard of a cricketer getting into trouble? Whereas football ... maybe it was all the adulation they got; made them think they could get away with anything. Half the footballers in London probably had a criminal record, if you looked closely enough; had, or at least jolly well ought to have. And here were another lovely couple. Sharing digs, choice pair of rotten apples. The Irish boy who likes to pick fights and the coloured boy who couldn't get it into his head that No meant No. That girl had been in an awful state. Three to five years, thought the detective-sergeant, given the current climate of sentencing.

The police were very correct with Brendan Domingo. Even if the barman at the Albion didn't know who he was, they did. Don't lay a finger on him, whatever you feel like. This case is going to get publicity enough by itself. We'll even call him sir for a bit; until we've charged him, that is. We'd like you to come with us and make a statement sir. Brendan was very polite back. He thought he ought to ask for a solicitor, but he didn't know any solicitors, so he asked if he could telephone the Boss. Later, son, no problem, you can do it from the station; let's just get the statement over with first, then you can call whoever you like. Brendan said OK, and went with them, wondering how long it would be before Danny and Mrs Ferris realised that when he'd said he'd had a bit of a fight, it was only in a manner of speaking.

Yes he knew someone called Maggie. No he didn't

know her surname. No he hadn't known her long. Yes, that was correct, they had met last night in the Albion for the first time. Yes, he had been to her flat. Yes, he had had sexual intercourse with her. Yes, it had been with her consent.

'How did you get those marks on your face?'

'She scratched me.'

'Scratched you quite a lot from the look of it.'

'Yes.'

'I see. And did you at any time while you were in her flat assault her?'

'Assault her? No.'

'Did you hit her at any point?'

'Yes, I hit her a few times,' said Brendan quietly.

'Why did you hit her?'

'Because she asked me to.'

'Because she asked you to?' The detective-sergeant looked across at the officer who was making notes of the interview. We've got a cheeky one here, he thought. Bold as brass.

'Yes.'

'And why ever should she ask you to do a thing like that?'

'I don't know. It seemed to be … her thing.'

'Her … thing?'

'Yes, well we were in bed you see, and she asked me to …'

'You were in bed with her at the time?'

'Yes.'

'You didn't hit her before you raped her? You just hit her while you were raping her?'

'I didn't rape her. I didn't rape her. I only hit her because she asked me to. It seemed to be … her thing.'

'You hit her when she refused to have sex with you, that's what you're saying, is it?'

'No, that's not what I'm saying at all. I ... I liked her.' It sounded pathetic, but Brendan felt he had to say it. It was part of the truth, and if he told them the truth they'd be bound to understand sooner or later.

'You liked her?'

'Yes. Course I did.'

'She's got a broken nose, severe bruising to the left side of the face, and one of her molars is loose. If that's what you do when you like people, sunshine, I wonder what you'd do if you fell in love with them.'

A broken nose? Christ.

'I only slapped her a few times. Because she asked me to,' he repeated.

'Apart from the head-butt.'

'The what?'

'The head-butt. Come off it, Brendan, that's what you footballers are good at, isn't it – the head-butt? Wait till the ref's looking the other way and then in with the nut. It may not be a criminal offence when you're playing for Athletic, but I can assure you it's against the law anywhere else.'

'I didn't butt her. She got hold of my ears and pulled my head into her face.'

'And the sun shines out of my arse.'

'It's true, she got hold of my ears and pulled my head on to her face.'

'Hard enough to break her nose?'

'I suppose so. If that's what happened.'

'That's what happened. Now you tell me, Brendan: why ever would she want to do a thing like that?'

'I don't know. She just ... did it. I don't know.'

'You see, son, we can help you a bit. Not much, but a bit. I mean rape's a very serious charge, especially nowadays, what with all the hoo-ha about it. A few years ago you might just have been able to get away with something like this, assuming you hadn't knocked her around so much, and assuming you'd thought up a better story. But as it stands, we're looking at five years, old son. Five to seven, I'd say. And that's not going to be too good for the old career, is it?'

Brendan looked down at the table. He somehow hadn't thought about not playing again. He'd thought about everything else, but he somehow hadn't thought about not being allowed to play football again. He didn't think he could stand it.

'So if I may offer a word, Brendan, I think we'd better go for the truth in the present instance. You just tell us what happened, and we'll do the best we can for you.'

Brendan didn't say anything.

'I suppose she was a bit of a tease,' said the detective-sergeant. 'Led you on a bit?'

'No,' said Brendan, 'she didn't.'

'This is hopeless.'

'Can I ring the Boss?'

'Later, Brendan.'

'Isn't it my rights to ring the Boss?'

'I don't think so, Brendan. I don't know where it's written down if it is. Do you know where it's written down if it is?'

Brendan shook his head.

'Perhaps we should ask the other officer?'

Brendan and the detective-sergeant looked across at the other officer, who had remained silent throughout the interrogation. He didn't speak this time, either, but merely shook his head slowly from side to side.

'No, he doesn't think it's written down either.'

Brendan was confused. The police didn't believe him, that was obvious; but they were being almost nice to him. Well, fair, anyway. They hadn't hit him, or called him a black bastard, or told him to go back to the trees. He remembered an incident from last season, only his second game for Athletic, playing away up north, and someone had thrown a banana on to the pitch right near him. If he could have found that fan, he might have head-butted him. But apart from the odd yellow card, he'd always stayed out of trouble on the pitch; took a bit of stick, dished some out, but never tried to do anyone deliberately. Stayed out of trouble off the pitch, as well. Until this. Just when everything seemed to be going a bit right.

They took him into a small room, told him to strip and left him. He sat around in his underpants for half an hour until the police doctor arrived. The doctor told him to remove his underpants, then had a good look at him. All over. Neither of them said a word as the doctor went about his business, occasionally stopping to make a note. He was particularly interested in Brendan's face, his ribs, and his cock. Why is he looking at my whatsit like that, thought Brendan. I haven't denied what we did. Perhaps the doctor was queer or something. Brendan felt weary, and also felt that nothing would surprise him any more.

Eventually, the doctor spoke.

'You can get dressed again now.'

After an hour or so, he was taken back to the two detectives. Again, the same one spoke. The other one was for beating you up, Brendan supposed.

'Well, this is a sorry mess.'

'Yes.'

'I bet you're wondering how you got yourself into it.'

Brendan didn't think that was a question, so didn't reply.

'I said I'm sure you're wondering how you got yourself into this?'

'Yes.'

'Well, let me give it a guess for you, Brendan. You picked up this girl in the pub, you thought that was a good start; she invited you in for coffee, you thought that was the green light; you had a bit of a kiss and a cuddle, she said it was a bit late, you said never too late for this, darling; she said No, you thought she meant Yes; she said No again, you hit her a bit and she hit you back, then you head-butted her and she went quiet, and because she didn't say anything you thought, Well if she isn't saying No she must mean Yes, and then you had your way with her. Give or take a few details which you'll now correct me on. Am I right or am I right?'

'I didn't pick her up; we just got talking. She didn't invite me in for coffee; she didn't even have any. She didn't say No or Yes or anything; it wasn't like that. I never hit her at all except when she ... she told me to.'

'Well, Brendan, I can't say you're being exactly cooperative. At the moment we've got rape and grievous bodily harm, and when we've looked over the girl's flat we may find we've got burglary as well, and if we can't have that we might settle for attempted burglary just to make up the three. I always like to charge in threes, you know; it's sort of neater, somehow. So you go away, my son, and you sit in a nice room for a few hours with a constable to keep you company, and you give your big woolly head a shake, and then you can come back and see me and I'll charge you.'

Brendan had wondered when they would get around to the fact that he wasn't the same colour as his interviewers.

'And then can I phone the Boss?'

'Then you can phone the Boss. If you think the Boss wants to hear from you after what you've been up to.'

In the end Brendan didn't phone the Boss. By the middle of Sunday afternoon, when Mrs Ferris had called the station for the third time and been told that Mr Domingo was still helping them with their inquiries, Danny Matson rang the Boss. Jimmy Lister got round to the station at six o'clock but was not allowed to see his player. No, he's still helping us with our inquiries, though all Brendan had done for the last three hours was stare at a radiator and wonder why Maggie had behaved the way she had. When Jimmy Lister mentioned that he'd be back in half an hour with a solicitor, the police said that was absolutely fine with them, but wasn't it a bit much getting a solicitor out on a Sunday night when nothing more was going to happen until the morning? If Mr Lister brought a solicitor along at ten, they could both be present when Mr Domingo was charged. How do you know he's going to be charged? He'll be charged all right, said the desk sergeant. You should have seen the state of that girl. He'll be charged even if he can prove he was in Alaska last night.

By the time Jimmy Lister returned with his solicitor, Duffy was off following a small idea. It was one of several small ideas he'd had, all of them so far useless; the trouble was, there weren't any big ideas around at the moment. All the questions that were there when he started sharing Jimmy Lister's salary were still no nearer solution. Why should anyone want to put Danny Matson out of the game? Why should anyone want to do down Melvyn Prosser? Why should anyone want to see the club relegated? And those three Whys were accompanied, naturally, by three Whos. Six questions, no answers. It was like arm-wrestling with Mr Joyce: you couldn't get past twelve o'clock, and the marmalade sandwich seemed inevitable.

Had Mr Joyce something to do with it? Was the Red White and Blue Movement backing Mr Bullivant and his Layton Road residents in some way? Was some other club trying to strong-arm its way out of the relegation zone by putting the heat on Athletic? That seemed a bit far-fetched. It couldn't just be that someone wanted to buy Brendan Domingo and was hoping to pick up a bargain at the end of the season when Athletic would be desperate for cash? Brendan was a good player, very honest, Duffy thought, and skilful for a big man; but he wasn't an undiscovered genius. Duffy doubted if he was even First Division material. What else? Perhaps he needed to ask Melvyn Prosser a few questions about the club's finances or something – assuming Melvyn Prosser was still giving him the time of day. That was the trouble. Football clubs were very public in some ways, but very private about backstage matters; they didn't need to tell anyone anything, and they usually chose not to as a matter of principle. BOARDROOM RESHUFFLE AT CITY you would read; but unless someone had been garrotted in the directors' box before several witnesses nothing ever came out. People retired 'for reasons of health'; new positions were created 'to give the Board a more effective cutting edge'; the chairman was changed 'to bring in some fresh blood'; and after six months or so everyone had forgotten, and there were a few embittered men in cashmere coats scattered around the district who could tell you a story if you had the time. But most people didn't have the time.

At the town hall they told him to follow the signs. Through the gloomy bits of Victorian Gothic, out into a courtyard, across some asphalt to a purpose-built sixties block: the planning department. The members of the public who got this far tended to be nuisances: that's to say, they actually wanted to check up on things that the planning department was doing, or was about to do, or had done. The planning department couldn't send them away – it had its statutory obligations; but there were times when public consultation and democratic access to files were simply other ways of saying the word time-wasting. Still, at least this character in the green suede blouson seemed to know what he wanted.

The assistant planning officer brought him the file. And there it was: an application for outline planning permission for an area covering the whole of the Athletic ground and two adjoining sites. The drawings which Duffy slowly unfolded showed a clean and stylish future for the place where the Layton Road enders currently stomped: a shopping mall, a leisure centre, an eight-storey block of flats with offices underneath; fully grown trees, fountains, zig-zag black-and-white pavements. Even some swanky, architect-designed pigeons taking off into the sky.

'Christ,' said Duffy.

'That *is* what you're looking for?' confirmed the assistant planning officer. She was amused, even gratified, by Duffy's reaction. Normally people just held the drawings upside down and grunted.

'Can you tell me what this means?'

'Well, it means that outline planning permission has been applied for.'

'How soon could they build this?'

'That's a long question. This is just a first step. It's an essential step, but it's only a first one. This is just for outline. That has to be granted, then there's full planning permission, and that has to be granted.'

'But basically, the club just gets one of these, then one of the next ones, and then goes ahead and knocks itself down and builds this instead?'

'Sort of. I mean, there might have to be a public inquiry; it depends on the project and whether there are any objections. But in any case I don't think this has anything to do with the club.'

'Eh?'

'Well, the application's in the name of Hess House Holdings. Unless that's the company name of the football club, which I shouldn't think it is.'

'Tell me if I'm following you. Someone can apply for planning permission to develop land which they don't in fact own?'

'Oh, yes.'

'So I could put in an application to turn Buckingham Palace into a gay club and the application would be duly received and considered?'

'You might have a problem with Crown Lands, but in principle the answer is Yes.'

'Why would I want to do such a thing?'

'I don't know. I'd have thought there were enough gay clubs anyway.' She smiled rather unenthusiastically at Duffy. Even some of the sensible ones were nutters.

'No, I mean, what are the advantages in terms of planning?'

'Well, it would speed things up. That's why most people apply for planning permission on land they haven't yet bought. It sort of primes the pump. Means you can start work as soon as the change of ownership comes through.'

'What else would they have to do at this stage?'

'Well, this is a big scheme. There'd obviously have to have been some consultations with council officers first. You know, fire, access, drainage. They'd have to have some idea of what might be allowable.'

'Private consultations?' Duffy heard the rustle of fat bribes.

'Private? Of course. There's nothing sinister about that. It's quite normal.'

'Sorry, I wasn't suggesting any irregularity.' Duffy was trying to work out how far some operator could get without anyone sniffing what he was up to. 'And how long would it be before any of this would be bound to become public knowledge?'

'Hard to tell. It depends a bit on the planning department's schedule of meetings. Things are always a bit slow in the summer. I'm only guessing, but I'd say we'd have to publish this scheme in, what, three or four weeks' time.'

Just after the end of the season. Neat.

'And how long would it take from the present stage to laying the first brick?'

'Couldn't tell you. Depends on too many things.'

'But if, say, things went really smoothly. Say there weren't any objections. Could they get a lot done in … three months?' June to September, the summer lay-off. Even the yobbos were away, kicking heads in Ibiza. Cor, look, Wayne, someone's nicked the Athletic ground while we've been away. So they cowing have.

'You could probably get through a lot of the paperwork, yes.'

The next stop was Companies House, City Road,

where they assumed Duffy was an investigative journalist from a radical underground paper. Up to a few years ago you always used to get respectably dressed people who knew what they wanted. Nowadays you got any old – or, worse, young – crackpot walking in, wanting this, wanting that. 'Hello, I'm from the *Monthly Paranoid*, we're a bit short on city scandal this issue, can you dig me out a nice conflict of interests, please?' – it was almost as bad as that.

Duffy flipped through the microfilm catalogue, paid his pound, and waited half an hour in the search room until his microfiche came through. Hess House Holdings. Registered 1974. Registered Office, Hess House W3. List of Directors. Dee-dum, dee-dum, Duffy read. Dee-dum dee-dum, dee-dum dee-dum. And then, well, well, well, Mrs C. R. Magrudo. He checked the profits as an afterthought. No profits declared for the last two years.

When he phoned Jimmy Lister that afternoon the Boss sounded rather far away.

'I think I've got something, I definitely think I might have got something,' said Duffy.

'Oh, yes. Crown Jewels turn up?'

'I won't tell you what it is now. I'd rather come round and see you.'

'Oh yes.'

'Is that all right?'

'Sure it's all right. But whatever you've got, Duffy, it won't make any difference. They just charged big Brendan with rape.'

Jimmy Lister ought to have been out on the pitch with the lads planning free kicks or something at the time Duffy arrived; but he was still sitting at his desk, mournfully waiting for the next bad thing to happen.

'It's all over,' he said, as Duffy sat down opposite him, 'it's just all fallen apart. First Danny, then Brendan, now the residents have got their injunction ...'

'When did they get that?'

'First thing this morning. Layton Road entrance closed till the end of the season. Leave to appeal granted, but not until it's too late. It's all over, Duffy. The club's going down the U-bend. You should have seen the lads this morning when I told them about Bren. End of the world, they knew it. And I don't think my glorious reign of management here is exactly going to bring the offers flooding in from Abu Dhabi.'

'How's he taking it?'

'Bren? Not too badly in a funny sort of way. I mean he says he didn't do it. *Course* he didn't do it – I know Bren like I know my own boy. He just seems to think that if he goes on saying he didn't do it, they're bound to believe him in the end. What he doesn't realise is that if he carries on saying he didn't do it they'll end up thinking he's being cheeky.'

'When does he come up?'

'Well, tomorrow, first time. Then there'll be a remand, then another remand, and so on.'

'Any chance of bail?'

'Not much, the solicitor said. Not nowadays. You know what the headlines are like – ACCUSED RAPIST FREE TO STALK THE STREETS, and all that. Even with Brendan always being a good boy, I don't think they'd do it.'

'If we got him bail, would you play him?'

'Come off it, Duffy. No way. No way. It wouldn't be fair on the lad. It just wouldn't be fair. Can you imagine what they'd do to him from the terraces? They'd roast the boy. I mean, remember Bobby Moore.'

Duffy remembered. The 1970 World Cup, the England captain, an incident in a jeweller's on another continent, and all the next season when he walked out on to the pitch he heard the tune of 'Clementine', and the fans singing, 'Where's the bracelet, where's the bracelet, where's the bracelet, Bobby Moore?' And he was as innocent as the breeze.

'I couldn't play the lad, Duffy. I don't know what I'd be more scared of, the fans away from home or the loyal supporters at the Layton Road end. He'd get crucified.'

'When do you see him next?'

'Tomorrow, next day. I'm not sure. I mean, it's obviously not just a club matter, it's a family matter as well. I can't go stomping in saying Please can I have my Bren back when there's his old mum sobbing her eyes out and seeing her boy getting set for five or six years behind bars.'

'When you see him, find out the name of the girl and where she lives.'

'What for?'

'Just find it out, Jimmy.' Lister was surprised by Duffy's attitude; it had suddenly become very businesslike. This wasn't altogether surprising. The more things that went wrong for Jimmy, the more things there were for Duffy to work on.

'Isn't that breaking the law or something? I mean, isn't there a big thing about protecting the anonymity of rape victims?'

'That's only about publishing her name in the papers. Look, you don't think Bren did it, do you?'

'No,' said Jimmy Lister, though in truth he thought Bren might have done it.

'Nor do I,' said Duffy, though as a matter of professional principle he never put anything past anybody. 'So if we know he's innocent, we've got to find why he's being fitted up, haven't we?'

'If you say so.'

'Get me her name, get me where she lives. Either from Brendan, or from the solicitor. They'd probably have to tell him if he asked.'

'All right, Duffy. I was going to say, please can I have my salary back; but I reckon I'm not earning it, so you may as well.'

'Ta. Now, is the chairman about?'

Melvyn Prosser was standing by his desk in his overcoat, just as before. This time, however, he didn't look like a businessman in a hurry; he looked like a sea-captain whose ship is going down, and who thinks the best way of handling it is to put on his pea-jacket.

'Still with us, Mr Duffy? Isn't it all a bit out of your hands now?'

'Parts of it, I expect. But I think I might be on to something.'

'Some magic way of getting us three points from each of our last six games?'

'Wish I could, Mr Prosser, wish I could. No, I don't know what made me think of it ...' He looked at Melvyn Prosser carefully as he said the next words. 'But I found out about the planning permission.'

Melvyn Prosser's broad, fleshy face with the vertical scar on the forehead disclosed to the keen observer only that Melvyn Prosser was still worried stiff about Brendan Domingo.

'What planning permission?'

'Did you know about the application for outline planning permission for the whole of the Athletic ground and two adjoining sites in Meadow Lane?'

'No, I didn't, Duffy. What sort of thing are we talking about?'

'Big development. Shopping centre. Offices, flats. Leisure centre.'

'Sounds like a good idea,' said Melvyn Prosser evenly. 'Sooner they wipe this shambles off the map the better.'

'Hey, *chief*,' Jimmy Lister protested.

'Sorry, Jim boy, you know how much I love this club. I love the game, I love the club. I'd do anything for this club, but you can't help getting a bit discouraged, sometimes.'

'Sure, chief.'

'I mean, don't think I overvalue my contribution. Any club – it's the players, it's the team, isn't it? The players, the fans, that's what counts. And the results. You can't have a happy club if you aren't getting the results. But I've always been right behind this club, and any little something I've been able to do, I've done.'

'Course you have, chief, course you have. Pulled the club up by its bootstraps.'

'No, no, I've just done what any other chairman would have done in my place.'

Like pay all the bills, Duffy thought. Like pay Jimmy Lister's wages, and thus, indirectly, mine. Duffy noticed that in Melvyn Prosser's basic outline of a football club no mention was made of the manager's role. He wondered if Jimmy Lister had noticed this.

'Anyway, Mr Prosser, shall I go on?' Duffy felt that the excitement of his discovery was being rather deflated by Melvyn Prosser's philosophising.

'Oh, go on, yes, sure.'

'Outline planning permission for the entire Athletic ground and two adjoining sites has been applied for by a company known as Hess House Holdings.'

'Never heard of them,' said Prosser.

'Hess House Holdings have an interesting Board of Directors,' said Duffy. 'One of them is listed as Mrs C. R. Magrudo.'

'Charlie's wife?' Melvyn seemed delighted. 'Charlie's wife?' Then he burst out laughing. 'The cheeky bugger. Cheeky Charlie Magrudo. You've got to laugh, haven't you?'

'Why?'

'Why? Because it's one of Charlie's jokes. You sure there wasn't something else on the plan? Like a light-house or a pier or an airport or something?'

Duffy was a bit pissed off with Melvyn Prosser.

'Look, Mr Prosser, correct me if I'm wrong. Someone's trying to fuck up this club. I asked you if you had any enemies. You mentioned Charlie Magrudo. I find out that Charlie Magrudo, through his wife, has applied for outline planning permission on this site.'

'Yes I'm sorry to laugh, Mr Duffy,' said Prosser, and carried on laughing none the less. 'But what do you deduce from this?'

'That Charlie Magrudo is trying to fuck up this club to buy it cheap and develop it like he's asked for.'

'Hmm. Yes, I'm sorry not to take your theory with the seriousness it warrants, and do please watch your language by the way, we're not in the team bath now. The point is, Charlie Magrudo hasn't got two beans to rub together.'

'What do you mean?'

'If he wanted to rub beans together, he'd have to take out his sole surviving bean and cut it in half first. He's a bankrupt. Not officially, of course, but as close as you can get without the men coming round for your three-piece suite at eight o'clock in the morning. That's why Mrs

Charlie's name's on everything. She holds the surviving bean in her little bean-bag, and takes it out occasionally and lets poor old Charlie count it.' Melvyn was off into chuckling again.

'You did him some naughty, you said, over some contract.'

'Oh, that. No, that wasn't much; just normal business procedure. The real naughty I did Charlie was with Mrs Charlie, and that was years ago. It's all blood under the bridge and I'm sure we've forgiven one another.'

'What was that bit of naughty?'

'Oh, you don't have to ask, do you? What do you do with your middle stump?'

'Sorry.'

'Not very bright today, are we? Look, the point about Charlie Magrudo is that if this whole club came up for sale he might, if the bank gave him a loan – which is less than likely – be able to bid for a half-share in the toilets. Maximum.'

'Couldn't he ... I don't know, get backing or something?'

'Not with Charlie's business record.'

'But ... but I read his file down at the *Chronicle*. They said he was a thriving local businessman.'

'I'll tell you how he does that. It's called buying the reporter a drink. It's called not turning up with dandruff on your collar. It may, or it may not, be called passing the wine list across to the reporter with twenty-five quid inside it – I wouldn't want to cast any aspersions on the lawfully wedded husband of Mrs Charlie or on the integrity of the gentlemen of the press.'

'Oh dear.'

'It's also called not believing what you read in the papers.'

'Oh dear. But why would he do it?'

'As I say, it's a typical Charlie joke. Well, it's typical of what he used to do, anyway. I haven't seen him for years, to tell you the truth. But it sounds like he's getting his own back for that little bit of council business I dropped him in. He puts in this plan, and then waits a bit, and then one day when he's a bit low or something, he gets someone to ring up the *Chronicle* and say, Did you know they were going to knock down the Athletic ground and build a racecourse? And they're bound to do a big story, whatever, aren't they? Front-page splash, if it's a boring week. And then Charlie gets to think about what my face will look like when I pick up the paper. Typical Charlie.'

'Oh dear.'

'Well, nice try, anyway,' commented Prosser benevolently. 'Uh-huh.'

As Duffy drove home, he thought, Typical. Bloody typical. Spend all morning chasing a really bright idea, find exactly what you're looking for, get back and what happens: something much more important has turned up, and your own bright idea is transformed into a real poodle.

Carol seemed to be coming round more often lately. Duffy couldn't work out whether this was because of him or her. Had he been asking her more, or had she been just turning up more? Perhaps those parts of her life he didn't like to ask about weren't so busy at the moment; perhaps Robert Redford was away on location and not able to ask her out so much. On the other hand, it might be that since his activities down at the Alligator were a bit curtailed at the moment, he'd been inviting her round more without noticing. Or it might be a mixture of the two.

'What're the chances of getting bail for rape nowadays?' he asked over dinner.

'Rape? Pretty thin. I mean, there's always a chance, because of the overcrowding in the cells. But it's not the sort of thing that happens very often. The bench doesn't like to get egg on its face, especially not with rape nowadays.'

'What if the accused has got a nice smile?'

'No previous?'

'None of any kind. Clean as a whistle. Simple conflict of evidence.'

'Well, it's possible. It's always possible. A smart lawyer might swing it. I mean, he might be able to suggest bail conditions that would satisfy the court.'

'Like having his cock chopped off?'

Carol grinned.

'I think they'd accept that.'

Duffy didn't think Brendan would, though. Then he noticed that Carol was looking at him and smiling. Oh dear, he thought: were things going to stop being neat again?

'You wash, I'll wipe.'

Carol sighed.

'You don't have to say it, Duffy. That's what we always do.'

Later, in bed, he realised that he hadn't worried about his lymph nodes all day. Well, that was something. Carol seemed wide awake, but Duffy had had enough. Another dog of a day. Another real bow-wow. As he lapsed into sleep, he remembered the last time Carol had stayed, and how he'd won himself a night sweat and an erection. The second of each. He could hear that man reading the sports results on the telly. Erections 2, Night Sweats 2. Replay on Monday.

When he woke up he realised that he'd got through the eight hours without a night sweat. He'd also got through the eight hours without an erection. Perhaps the two *were* connected in some way. Perhaps you couldn't have one without the other. That worried him.

There were four weeks of the season to go, and six games left for Athletic. Fourth from bottom of the table, and with everyone in the relegation zone having played the same number of games, their future was, as the lads kept telling one another and the manager kept telling the lads, in their own hands. If they won every single remaining match, they wouldn't be relegated. Of course; but you might as well say that if they'd won every single previous game in the season, they'd be in the Second Division by now. Who, for instance, fancied Athletic's chances away from home to top-of-the-table Oxford? That was the trouble at the end of a season. The clubs at the top were still chasing promotion, and you didn't expect any favours from them; while the clubs at the bottom were trying to escape the drop as much as you were. This left the clubs in the middle, the clubs who'd had an average season but were safe for another year. In theory this made them easy pickings: kick them about a bit in the first twenty minutes, and they lost interest and started to think about their summer holidays. But it didn't work out like that: just because they were safe for another year, they were more relaxed, more ready to try things, less depressed if they went a goal down. All footballers like to play a bit of fancy stuff if they can; they like to score goals; and they like to win matches. Middle-of-the-table clubs at the rear end of the season aren't any different in these basics. And if you tried kicking them, well, who likes being kicked, especially by some no-hoper with his luggage packed for the Fourth Division? Middle-of-the-tablers can kick back just as well; they might even mind a little less than you do about being sent off.

'Mr Bullivant, good morning.'

'You again, laddie, I thought they'd fired you.'

'Yes, well, you see, I'm still learning.' Duffy took out his notebook, uncapped his biro, and tried to look as if he were about to take down the Sermon on the Mount.

'Well, you can't come and practise on me every day.'

'How's the osteopathy going?' Duffy thought it a good idea to establish some rapport before asking his real questions.

'Very well, thank you.'

'How do you feel about getting the injunction?'

Bullivant didn't answer. Instead, he continued to stare at Duffy's notepad.

'You haven't written anything down yet, smiler. Aren't you going to write down that the osteopathy is going very well?'

'Oh, yes, sorry.' Duffy started writing, then looked up. Mr Bullivant was grinning at him.

'You're a real berk, aren't you?'

'Mr Bullivant, how do you feel about getting the injunction?'

'I would just like to say on this one, that British justice is the finest in the world, and you can quote me.'

'You think this will be the end of the trouble?'

'The British police are the finest in the world and I have every confidence that they will carry out the duties entrusted to them to the best of their ability. Write it down.'

Duffy wrote it down.

'Do you think you are in any way damaging the prospects of the club at this vital stage of the season by your actions?'

'Soccer hooliganism is a reflection of a wider violence which affects all parts of our society. You cannot merely consider soccer hooliganism by itself. You must look at the breakdown of respect for law and order generally, and the lack of self-discipline in a society that has gone soft. Going too fast for you?'

Duffy dutifully copied all this down, then read it through.

'What's that got to do with my question?'

'Just checking to see if you'd write down any old rubbish.'

'Mr Bullivant, will Mr Magrudo continue to support your action even if the club appeals and goes to a higher court?'

'How's that again?'

'Will Mr Magrudo continue to foot the bills if the club appeals?'

'Who's that?'

'Mr Magrudo.'

'Who does he play for? Italian World Cup squad?'

'Mr Bullivant, I happen to know that Mr Magrudo is paying your solicitor's bills.'

'Why would some Italian footballer pay my bills? Athletic aren't in the European Cup are they, or haven't I been reading my papers lately?'

'Mr Bullivant ...'

'You're a real berk, you know that? A real berk. Write it down. B.E.R.K., that's right. I think I like the yobbos more than I do you.'

'Well, at least you'll be able to plant flowers in your front garden, Mr Bullivant, now that the yobbos have gone.'

'Bye-bye, tulip,' said Mr Bullivant unexpectedly.

Well, that was another idea gone. Perhaps he should go over to Ealing to the house with the flagpole and ask Mr Joyce if he was being paid by Mr Magrudo. He'd be sure to tell him, too. Yes, Mr Magrudo the well-known near-bankrupt who just has enough money to buy himself flattering mentions in the local paper, yes as a matter of fact he is supporting the Red White and Blue Movement, and when he's built his nice new leisure centre with all the money he hasn't got he's going to let us have a recruiting booth outside and also a reviewing stand so that we can have march-pasts and he'll be giving us a lifetime's supply of toast and marmalade, you really are a berk, Mr – what was it you said your name was this time?

At least with Danny Matson he could be himself. Danny still had his foot up on the stool. Terrible about big Bren, wasn't it? Terrible. No, he hadn't seen or heard him come in. Must have been real quiet; unless it was late, of course. In the morning they – Danny and Mrs Ferris – had found him sitting downstairs at the breakfast table in his club blazer, club tie and best trousers. Just staring ahead of himself, frowning a bit, with these big scratches on his face. Said he'd been in a fight. Wouldn't say any more. Just sitting there, waiting. Ate his breakfast like normal; didn't want to talk about the game at all; just waiting. And then the coppers came. Yes, sure, he said. Will I need any clothes or anything, he said as they took him off. Poor Bren. Anything else? No, nothing else. Just wouldn't talk about it. He's a class player, you know that?

Class. Very nimble for a big fellow. Got it up here, too. Danny tapped the side of his head, indicating brains.

The Magrudo Construction Company turned out not to be quite as grand as its name. It was a small builder's yard off Copton Avenue, and yes, the receptionist was sure Mr Magrudo would be free some time before lunch if he didn't mind waiting. Mr Magrudo was always happy to see people from the *Chronicle*. Take a seat.

Charlie Magrudo arrived at about twelve in a four-year-old Granada which looked as if it stalled if it heard the word car-wash. Ten minutes, quarter of an hour, sure, no problem. He was a round, friendly man, dark hair, and rather tight in his suit; comfortable-looking, like some middle-rank snooker player who'd never quite made the top fifty, but was more than happy doing the rounds of the little clubs.

'We haven't met before, Mr Marriott?'

'No.'

'No. I've seen quite a bit of Ron down the years, Ron Grayson. And Gerry Douglas, of course. Old friends.' Old recipients of small bribes, thought Duffy. 'You new?'

'Newish. I'm sort of doing a bit of everything. Sports pages mainly, but they've also given me a few stories to do about planning, roadworks, things like that.'

Duffy tried to make it sound low-key. He also hoped that Charlie Magrudo wasn't a keen reader of bylines, in which case he might have known that Ken Marriott had been on the sports desk for four years, and never once gone near the other pages.

'So how can I be of assistance? Always ready to help the gentlemen of the press.'

'It's about this application for a development on the site of the Athletic ground.'

'Yes, sure. What do you want to know?'

'How realistic would you say it was?'

Mr Magrudo thought it was very realistic. He gave Duffy a run-down on the plans as if he'd been going through them only that morning with the architect, and was shortly off for a working lunch with an American bank to clean up the last details of the financing. He gestured a lot, and as he talked his hands seemed to create the shopping centre, the eight-storey block of flats, the piazza, the fountains, the trees in tubs, the lively bustle of a successful commercial project. Duffy thought it all sounded wonderful; but he also thought it time he added to Ken Marriott's academic qualifications.

'Mr Magrudo, I hope you don't think this impertinent of me ...'

'Fire away. Ask me the hard questions. Be my guest.'

'Well, before I did my three-year planning course, I read economics at university. Now I expect I'm a bit rusty, but I'd say we're looking at a project high in seven figures, maybe even eight. It sounds a splendid idea, even if it does mean Athletic losing their ground and having to look for a new one. But the hard question I have to ask is this. You don't even own the site yet, and I simply don't see how you can raise the money.'

Charlie Magrudo was about to answer, but Duffy went swiftly on. He didn't want to get Charlie blustering and then forced to defend an indefensible position. There would be more chance of the truth if Duffy played it a bit tough. In the nicest possible way, of course.

'You see I've had a little look at Magrudo Construction and its associates. It's a very solid little family firm, if you don't mind my saying so. You'll be able to change that Granada for a new model this year or next, I should say. But we're talking seven figures just for the site, Mr Magrudo, and I couldn't help noticing at City Road that you haven't declared for the last couple of years. Now that's not on. In fact it's so much not on that, if you don't mind my saying so, I think it must all be about something else.'

Charlie Magrudo spread his hands and smiled.

'They would send you, wouldn't they? I mean, just my luck to get the brainiest fellow on the *Chronicle*. If they'd sent Ron or Gerry, I reckon I could have done enough pulling of the wool. Look if I don't say another word, have you got a story?'

'Sorry, no.'

'Not even a paragraph? A paragraph? We could have lunch about it?'

'Sorry. I'm afraid it's either a big story or it's nothing. It seems to me it isn't a big story any more; it's just a question of whether you want to tell me what it's all about, though there's absolutely no reason at all why you should.'

'Fair cop,' said Charlie, 'fair cop. I just hoped it might work. It's a joke, actually.'

'A *joke*?' Duffy really put on the amazement. Anything to let Magrudo know that his plan was at least causing some reaction.

Then Charlie told him about Melvyn Prosser, and old rivalries of a kind which were sometimes friendly and sometimes a little less friendly. The name of Mrs Magrudo, Duffy noticed, did not come up. The version of events concerning the council contract was also a little different from Melvyn Prosser's. But the story was essentially the same.

'How did you think Mr Prosser would react?'

'Well, I hoped that for one minute, just for one minute or even less, he'd be scared shitless,' said Charlie Magrudo. 'I just had this picture of him opening his paper and thinking his lovely new football club which he was so proud of was going to be bulldozed down and concreted over. I just wanted him to be scared shitless. Perhaps even for longer than a minute.'

'Do you think he would have believed it?'

'He might have. He might have. I mean, we haven't seen each other for quite a few years now. He might have thought I'd done some good business, made a little pile, and was just about to come bursting in all over him.'

'Well, I'm sorry to have spoiled your joke, Mr Magrudo.'

'Oh, don't worry. It was a bit of a long-shot. What did you say your name was?' .

'Marriott. Ken Marriott.'

'Nice meeting you, Ken. We must have that lunch some time.'

'I'd like that, Mr Magrudo.'

'Charlie from now on, son. Tell you what, I think you'll go far in your chosen profession.' And Mr Magrudo gave him a big wink.

Well, that was another door closed in Duffy's face. Sometimes it seemed to him that there were more doors closing than had ever been open in the first place. Still, at least Mr Magrudo thought he was a good journalist. Duffy quite wanted to get Charlie Magrudo and Mr Bullivant together and listen to the pair of them discussing the merits of Ken Marriott, *Chronicle* journalist. He'd like to have Maggot listening in on the conversation as well.

All he could do now was push on the only door left that was slightly ajar. The next day Jimmy Lister, with some reluctance, released to Duffy the name of Maggie

Coleman, and the address off Twyford Avenue. Duffy realised he had to play this one very carefully indeed. If there was one thing the coppers didn't like it was outsiders coming in and hassling rape victims. They got very cross about that sort of thing. There were a few sections of the criminal law especially designed to deter people from leaning on prosecution witnesses; and the coppers certainly wouldn't mind using them. Much as he liked Brendan, Duffy wasn't ready to join him in the next cell just yet. So he started low-key. He started by ringing Geoff Bell.

'Atom sub 24 degrees south 22 degrees east request permission instant destroy query PM waiting urgentest.'

'Hallo, Duffy,' said Geoff. 'That was a bit over the top even for you. Is it about the match on Sunday?'

'Wondered if you'd be interested in a little photographic assignment?'

'Very nice.'

'It's pretty difficult, actually, Geoff. I mean, there are certain aspects to it which could turn tricky.' You always had to do this with Bell. He couldn't get interested in easy assignments, somehow; you always had to dress them up. Duffy found it a bit tiresome.

'Try me.'

Duffy tried him, emphasising the possibility that there might be an incredible number of plain-clothes men around, that Maggie Coleman might be living locked in her flat with the curtains drawn, and so on.

'Leave it with me,' said Geoff. 'Oh, and Duffy?'

'Yes?'

'Those coordinates are all to cock. Who'd put an atomic sub in the middle of the Kalahari Desert?'

'I'll do better next time, Geoff.'

There was another thing he could do when the doors were closing in his face. He didn't like doing it, but he somehow always fell back on it. He asked Carol to check out three names for him on the police computer: Maggie Coleman, Charlie Magrudo and Melvyn Prosser. Carol always said No, and Duffy bullied her a bit, and then she finally said Yes, and they both got a bit silent. Duffy always felt bad, but there it was. He tried being as nice as he could to Carol afterwards, but she remained silent and a bit distant; she stayed the night, but there weren't any cuddles. No cuddles, no swollen cocks, and no night sweats.

On the Saturday Athletic were away to Oxford, and Duffy turned on the radio to catch the result. Oxford 2 Athletic 1. Oxford now assured of promotion, Athletic drop back into the bottom three. Pitch invasion by Oxford fans, some scuffles when travelling Athletic fans come on to the pitch as well. Eighteen arrests, one policeman slightly injured.

'It was a sickener,' said Jimmy Lister at the ground next morning. 'The lads really did their stuff. I mean there we were, biggest crowd of the season, ten thousand or so I'd say, a real promotion–relegation number, and this Brendan business hanging over their heads. They really battled, those lads. Came in one–nil down at half-time, none of them needed lifting, we had a little talk and thought if we could match them a bit more in midfield and then get just a good bounce of the ball, there wasn't any reason why we shouldn't share the points. I was really impressed by the lads' attitude. It was as if they were doing it for Bren. It was funny, no one mentioned his name, not once, but I'd lay money that every one of us on the coach had been thinking about big Bren all locked up in his little cell. In a funny sort of a way, it seemed to bring out the best in the lads.

'Second half, they really did the club proud. Got hold of the midfield, lots of pressure, and we nicked one back after twenty minutes. Not the cleverest goal we've ever scored, but a goal we deserved all the way. I really did think the lads would do it then. I really thought if they got one, there's no reason why they can't get another. Or at least come away with a result. What happens? Ten minutes to go, the lads pushing up in search of a winner, breakaway goal. Not even trying to play the offside trap, just caught a tiny bit square and their number eight was straight through. Speedy little bastard. What a sickener.'

'Still, it sounds as if they've got the right attitude, at least.'

'Bags of character, Duffy. Maybe I've been wrong all season. You know how I like to get teams to play. Maybe that was wrong. They'll never be very fancy on the ball, this lot, but they've got guts hanging out of their ears. I just should have recognised it earlier.'

'Don't blame yourself, Jimmy. What do you think the chances of staying up now are?'

'Worse than they were before. I mean, it's not just up to us any more, is it? We've got to rely on one or two of the others slipping up as well. Just got to keep battling, haven't we? Just got to keep battling.' Jimmy Lister wondered gloomily what they did to you in Abu Dhabi if they caught you with the physio's wife. Chopped it off, most likely.

On Sunday the players who had been hurt the previous afternoon came in to see the physio for treatment. Duffy wandered down to the physio's room to the echo of Jimmy's words. Keep battling. Good attitude. Guts hanging out of their ears. It was odd to hear the elegant England B international of ten years ago coming out with all the old football manager's clichés. But there was truth in them, even so. They expressed what Athletic had to do for the next five games. No point doing anything else. It was also what Duffy would have to do, because Duffy's position was no more promising than Athletic's. He just had to keep on battling and hope for a bloody great brainwave. Or a bloody great stroke of luck. Or both at the same time, thank you very much.

Throughout this business Duffy had felt a bit like the goalkeeper he was. He felt useful, but only in a defensive way. All goalkeepers have spells of envying the outfield players – they want to rush out of the area, surge upfield and have a kick at the opposing net. But they're stuck, penned into their neat little box, their square-cornered territory: you're doing a nice job, let's leave it that way, don't get ideas above your station. Keepers only get a crack at the other side's net when they're allowed to take penalties: Duffy, for all his occasional hints, had yet to be entrusted with a spot kick by the Reliables.

There was, however, a freak way in which a goalkeeper could score: Duffy had seen it happen once on television. The keeper advances to the edge of his box and gives the ball a bloody great hoof; a following wind catches it and whisks it further than anyone had anticipated; it fools the defenders, bounces, catches the opposing keeper too far off his line, and lobs over his head into the net. Incredibly lucky, of course: it depended on a strong boot, a helpful breeze, a lethargic defence and a rash goal-minder. But it could happen. It was the sort of break Duffy needed in the present business; very much indeed.

Saturday's injuries had been light: one aggravated groin strain plus one slightly ricked knee.

'Not bad for this stage of the season,' commented Reg Palmer the physio. 'Normally you get a lot of extra little tears and niggles, especially with the older players.' He strapped a tension bandage on a midfielder's knee. 'All the injuries seem to be happening off the park for some reason.'

Duffy hung around, waited until the two players had been patched up, and chatted away to Reg Palmer. He was a thin, wiry man of uncertain years and terrifying fitness. He had been at the club for thirty years. Seen it all. Managers come and go. Promotion, relegation, good players, bad players, pitches all over the country and injuries all over the body. Boardrooms come and go, yes, that too.

'What was it like before Mr Prosser arrived?'

'Oh, it was all right. Bit of a shambles; no one quite knew who was giving the orders. It's a bit clearer under Mr Prosser.'

'Has he made changes?'

'Well, he brought Jimmy in, didn't he? And it's always nice having someone new, isn't it? Full of enthusiasm, especially at first. Offered me all sorts of machines – you know, sonic whatsits, infrared and all that. Happy to spend quite a bit on the physio room, if I wanted it. But I said No, I'll stay with God's two hands and my bag of tricks. Still, it was a nice offer.'

'Does he – I don't know – does he interfere much?'

'Interfere? Not that I've noticed. One thing he does do is ring me every Sunday afternoon, four o'clock, without fail, and ask me exactly what lads I've got under treatment and how they're getting on. Most chairmen would think they were a bit too grand for that, but not Mr Prosser. He may not get their names right, but he does ask after them.'

'Is he popular?'

'Yes, he's popular. I mean, every club's got to have a chairman, haven't they? I've known quite a few, and I've known far worse. No, Mr Whatever-your-name-is,' and Reg Palmer looked sternly at Duffy, 'you won't hear anything against Mr Prosser from me.'

'I wasn't asking, Mr Palmer. I just wondered. I was also wondering, if he's an improvement on what went before, then why is the club doing worse?'

'Well, he's not picking the team, is he? He's not picking and training the team.'

Or maybe Duffy wasn't looking to boot the ball hopefully upfield, see it catch a following wind and bounce over the opposing keeper's head. Maybe he wasn't looking to lean against a half-open door just in time to stop it shutting in his face. Maybe it wasn't a matter of battling away, showing bags of character, and having guts hanging out of your ears. Maybe it was more like seeing a little chink in a wall, and inserting a chisel or a screwdriver or something, and giving it a little twist, and watching the whole wall tumble down. The whole front wall of a shopping centre, leisure complex and block of offices-cum-flats, with or without the addition of piazza, fountains, tubbed trees, lighthouse, pier, airport, racecourse or whatever.

On the Monday morning he telephoned Hess House Holdings. This called for the posh voice.

'Jeremy Silverlight here. Is Mr Magrudo going to be in today? It's a touch urgent.'

'Hold the line, sir, please.'

Pause.

'He should be here about two thirty. Can I take any message?'

'No, I'll call again. Two thirty, you said?'

'Yes, sir.'

At ten minutes past two he rang Hess House Holdings again and asked to be put through to Charlie Magrudo's secretary. He didn't know if Charlie had a secretary at Hess House, but that didn't matter. The way these places operated, they usually made up a 'secretary' on the spot, especially if you sounded like money down the other end of the phone. They wouldn't say, 'Oh, Mr Magrudo hasn't got a secretary, actually the firm's not doing well enough for that, there is a girl somewhere who we think slept with Mr Magrudo – well, Charlie to all of us girls – but she's down the corridor putting nail varnish on a run in her tights at the moment so I'll get her to call you back when she's finished.' No, they wouldn't say that. What they would say is this:

'Trying to connect you.'

And after a minute or so (perhaps the girl was putting nail varnish on a run in her tights): 'Mr Magrudo's office.'

'Jeremy Silverlight. I gather Mr Magrudo's going to be with you shortly.'

'Yes, he's expected.'

'It isn't actually Charlie I want to get hold of. Well, I wouldn't mind a word, but that can wait. It's Mel Prosser. He's a devil to track down. His office thought he might be on his way to Hess House with Charlie. Do you know about that?'

'I'm afraid I don't.'

'Hmm. Look, sorry to be a pest, but perhaps you could check Charlie's book and see if he's expecting Mel this afternoon?'

Pause.

'There's nothing in the book, sir. Though of course that doesn't necessarily mean that ...' She sounded helpful as well as helpless.

'No, of course. Actually, I wouldn't put it past Mel to tell his office he was going to see Charlie when he was actually going somewhere else. He's more than a touch crafty, our Mel. Still, I don't want to bore you with the ins and outs of how old Mel Prosser carries on business. We could be here all night.' The rambling was deliberate, and the question it provoked was more or less forced.

'How can I help you, sir?'

'Look, I'm not going out of my tiny, I hope. I mean, correct me if I'm wrong, but Charlie does see quite a lot of Mel, doesn't he?'

'Oh, yes, sir. He's always round. Well, not always, but he's been round a lot lately. He just sort of drops in. That's why we don't really put him in the book.'

If there is a book, thought Duffy.

'Well if he does turn up, could you ask him to give me a bell on 205 3637. You've got the name?'

'Silverlight, yes sir.'

'I mean, don't bother if he doesn't turn up this afternoon. I can catch him at home in the evening.'

Phew. Being a bit posh down the phone always took it out of Duffy. And at the same time he felt a little surge of satisfaction. Is that the chink in the wall? And if so, which way do I turn the chisel?

Ten minutes later, the phone went. Duffy jumped, almost expecting it to be Melvyn Prosser. In a way, he wished he'd left his real number, just for a laugh.

'Watch the birdie.'

'Sorry?'

'Click, click, watch the birdie.'

'Oh, hello, Geoff. Sorry, wasn't concentrating.'

'You should have warned me about the lenses.'

'Geoff, I thought you were best left to work that out for yourself.'

'Well, you could have given me some idea. I mean, I needed at least the 200 and probably the 400, and there I was stuck with a piddly little 35 to 80 zoom on and I just had to decide, well do I shoot or do I change and I thought anything was better than nothing so I shot.'

'I think that was the right decision.'

'So I've got you some earlies, anyway, and I know the answer is not to have just the one camera body but three. I suppose in a way I'm as much to blame as you.'

'I'll be right round, Geoff.'

'Well, I warn you, I had some trouble blowing them up. And if you'd told me the flats faced west ...'

'I'm truly sorry.' Sometimes Duffy thought that Geoff was even more of a worrier than he was.

The photos, of course, were almost perfect, just what Duffy had asked for. They showed a girl with blonde hair emerging from a block of flats, looking around her, and setting off down the street. Pity about the dark glasses. He didn't know what sort of shape Maggie Coleman was in, but he always thought wearing dark glasses was the stupidest way of trying to go unnoticed. It just made you look like some Cabinet Minister's moll, or a star witness in a divorce case. 'And here, leaving her block of flats near Twyford Avenue, Acton, we see Maggie Coleman, the doctor's wife accused of administering a lethal dose of weedkiller to her husband, who has just been flown back to England by the Spanish authorities after vacationing in Marbella with Pedro the handyman.'

As against that, the glasses did make it harder to see what her face was like. Duffy spread out the photos and stared at them.

'Oh, and I did get this one, but I didn't really have time to focus, and with all that business of the lenses ...'

It was a sharp, well-focused picture of Maggie Coleman raising her glasses. You still couldn't see her eyes, because they were cast down, looking at something out of shot; but it was exactly the sort of photo Duffy wanted.

'I just got it in time. Lucky I changed the lens first, before I followed her. And then, even so, it was pure chance that I parked where I could see between a couple of vans. She took off the glasses to see if some fruit was ripe in the greengrocer's.'

'Does it look like her?' Duffy asked.

'What do you mean?'

'Well, would you say it was a good likeness?'

'Look, I'm sorry, if I'd known you wanted Lord Snowdon ...'

'Sorry, Geoff. Sorry. They're terrific, they're just what I wanted.'

'They may be just what you wanted, but they're not terrific. Technically, they're pretty much in the Third Division.'

It was always a bit like this with Geoff. He didn't care whether he was photographing a politician's moll, or a child murderer, or even some girl in the street that you fancied. He was only interested in whether he should have stopped down a bit more, or whether there was enough density in the negative. Look, Geoff, here's a picture of the entire Royal Family with no clothes on. I think they should have lit it more from the side, Duffy, and that crop is terrible.

'Thanks, Geoff. See you Sunday?'

'We're playing away.'

'So we are. Sorry.'

Duffy went first to the Albion, since that was where Brendan had picked Maggie up, or vice versa, depending on whether you were a policeman or one of the rare Athletic fans on his side. The barman who couldn't remember Brendan Domingo couldn't remember Maggie Coleman either. No; well, anyway, she can't be a regular, because I remember the regulars. But she was with a regular: she was with Brendan Domingo. Who's he? Brendan Domingo, he's the footballer I was in here asking about a couple of weeks ago, asking about the fellow in a mackintosh he'd been drinking with. Oh, the coloured fellow? That's right. No, he hasn't been back here since. What, the man in the mackintosh? No, the coloured fellow, the Brendan fellow, he hasn't been back since you first came and asked me about him. Why, he done something or something?

Hopeless. Duffy drove to the Athletic ground, waited until training was over, asked Jimmy Lister's permission, which he granted reluctantly, and showed the photos to the lads.

'That's her? The one who did Bren?'

'The one Bren did, you mean.'

'Tasty.'

'Wouldn't mind a bit.'

'Worth a year or two behind bars.'

'Always knew Brendan could pull them.'

'Where's she live, Duffy? You got her address?'

In a way, Duffy wasn't surprised. Footballers were very sentimental, but they were also pretty tough. They had to be to get through. Footballers in the first team couldn't afford to think about footballers who weren't in the first team. Healthy footballers couldn't afford to think about footballers whose legs had been broken, whose backs had given way, whose tendons had snapped. Footballers in form couldn't afford to think about footballers who had lost their form. Being a first-team player meant not being a lot of other things – like someone sitting in a purple chair with his leg up, or someone sitting in a cell with a bucket in the corner – and you couldn't let those other things get on top of you.

Kennie Hunt was the only one who thought there was something vaguely familiar about Maggie Coleman.

'Can't remember her, eh, Kennie? You can't have forgotten all the lucky ones.'

'I think I've seen someone like her.'

'Kennie just wants to keep the picture. Fancy her a bit, do you Kennie?'

'Any idea where you might have seen her?' asked Duffy.

'All the same in the dark to you, aren't they, Kennie?'

'Not sure. Maybe down at The Knight Spot.'

'Give him the picture, Mr Duffy, that's what he's after.'

'Hang on to one of these. See if it helps you remember.'

'That's what he wanted. Here, give us another look, Kennie.'

Duffy drove to The Knight Spot and rang the bell. Fat Frankie was no doubt still sleeping off his lagers, but Vince was there, in early, doing the books. Yes? Oh, any friend of Jimmy's, any friend of the Athletic. Vince was as worried as anyone about the chances of Athletic going down to the Fourth at the end of the season. Third Division footballers were OK, I mean close your eyes and they were almost in the Second Division, and that's class. But Fourth Division? Come to my wonderful fashionable west London club and gaze upon a special table of wallies who managed to get themselves relegated at the end of last season? Girls, get yourself picked up by the cream of the Fourth Division! It didn't sound much of a selling point to Vince.

The pictures? Well, we get a lot of girls in here. The thing about girls is, I don't really notice them unless they don't fit in somehow. You know, if they're too classy or too trampy. Otherwise, they all look the same. It must be the hair or something – you know, if they all dress the same and have the same hair, you can't tell them apart. Unless it's just that I'm getting old. It could be that. This one, for instance, this one you're showing me, she's very familiar. She is? Yes, she's very familiar because she looks like a thousand other girls. Not too trampy, not too classy. I wouldn't know her even if I'd passed the time of day with her a dozen times. I simply wouldn't know. Do you think Athletic have got any chance of staying up?

The trouble was, Duffy hadn't any idea where the best places to ask were. He didn't want to get too close to Twyford Avenue in case it got back to the coppers that someone whose credentials weren't exactly kosher was asking about Maggie Coleman. But if he stayed away from Twyford Avenue, where did he look? She'd met Brendan in the Albion, but that didn't necessarily mean she liked pubs. Even so, he tried the Bell and Clapper, the Rising Sun and the Duke of Cambridge. No go. Then he tried Benny's, where for a change they remembered Brendan, but where they had never seen the girl before. Then, as a long shot, he tried The Palm Tree, where a couple of sleepy West Indians shook their heads, and at the name of Brendan Domingo said, Brendan Domingo? Haven't seen him for a year or so, used to be a bit of a regular, gone to stay with the white folks since he's got so famous. Even if he does live just round the corner, he still prefers the company of the white folks.

So Duffy went just round the corner to see the white folks; or at least to see one of them – Danny Matson. As he walked into the tiny room with the purple chair, Duffy felt a bit depressed. Danny was still there, foot up, as cheerful as he could be, and pleased to see Duffy; but it was still depressing somehow. Depressing because here was a footballer who wasn't playing football. Duffy recalled the feelings of the Athletic players when shown Maggie Coleman's photo. Make a joke of it, lads, something like this could happen to you. Anything could go wrong at any time, remember that. Stay fit, play well, don't get into any trouble, and with a bit of luck you might stay off the scrap-heap until you are thirty-five. But there are a whole lot of junior scrap-heaps all the way along the line to thirty-five. Duffy couldn't understand why footballers didn't worry a lot more than they did. Or perhaps worrying was another thing that was bad for you: if you worried, you ended up on the worriers' scrap-heap, the scrap-heap kept specially for the indecisive footballer who dishes himself by thinking too much. Maybe you could only get to the top and stay at the top by having certain strong traits – single-mindedness, tenacity, cruelty – and cutting everything else out.

'This is a joke, Duffy?' said Danny Matson, looking serious.

'Eh?'

'This is a joke? You are pulling the one with bells on?'

'Come again?'

'This is the girl big Bren is supposed to have raped?'

'Yup. Maggie Coleman.'

157

'Oh. Maggie Coleman, eh? She told me she was called Denise.'

The trouble with putting a chisel into a wall and twisting is, of course, that the whole blade might break off. And that could be a great waste of time.

'Mr Prosser?'

'Oh. Still with us, Mr Duffy?'

'Wondered if I could have a word.'

'That usually means more than one. How long do you want?'

'Ten minutes?' Duffy really wanted twenty or thirty.

'That usually means twenty or thirty.' Prosser smiled. 'If you can find your own way back from north London you'd better come in the car with me.'

'Thanks.'

'Turn round.'

Duffy turned round.

'Lift your feet.'

Duffy raised first one foot, then the other, displaying the soles of his shoes to Mr Prosser.

'Right. Fine. Hop in. Only you can't be too careful, what with all the dogshit around nowadays.' Duffy rather liked Melvyn Prosser. Well, approved of, perhaps he meant. Well, sympathised with, perhaps. Well, recognised another neurotic when he saw one, that was nearest the truth.

'Drink?' Melvyn said, while Duffy was still awed by the amount of room in the back of the Corniche. As big as a hotel suite. Certainly as big as Danny Matson's room. Lovely carpet – I'd make them wipe their feet too. Gold upholstery. Telephone. Little control panel with buttons at Mr Prosser's elbow. Lovely. 'You don't get one of these in our society without treading on a few toes' – that's what Prosser had said. Whose toes?

'Tonic water, please. Lovely motor.'

'Thank you. Let's see, one tonic water.'

'Have you got Slimline?'

As Melvyn Prosser poured the tonic into a nice bit of cut glass, Duffy gazed at the carpet. Beige, with flecks of brown in it. Little flecks of brown. Was that what Kaposi's sarcoma looked like?

'Well you've had two minutes already.'

'What do you think of the lads' chances tonight?' At home to mid-table Wigan. Could be a difficult match. Thrashed four–nil up there in the early part of the season. Bound to remember that, some of the lads, that's what Jimmy Lister had said.

'You didn't ask for a lift all the way to Muzzie Hill where you aren't going in order to ask me that.'

'How much are you worth, Mr Prosser?'

'Ha ha. Yes. Well, I wish I knew. But it's the old saying, I'm afraid. I make the money, and I pay others to count it.'

'But we're talking well into six figures, aren't we, Mr Prosser? I mean, I'd say well into seven figures.'

'That's very generous of you.'

'You must be quite used to things being a success?'

Melvyn Prosser chuckled.

'I'm very glad I'm not footing your bill, Mr Duffy. I think it's very funny, the idea of Jimmy Lister paying you, what is it, fifty quid a day plus expenses to ride in the chairman's Corniche and ask him tricky questions. This is the bit, I suppose, where I say, Yes I am used to success and look all smug and pleased with myself and then you say something I wasn't expecting and I break down and admit I'm the Boston Strangler and Jack the Ripper and Colonel Gaddafi.'

'I'm not trying to ask you tricky questions. I'm just trying to get some background. For instance, there you are, rich man, used to success, and you find yourself with a real loser on your hands like the Athletic. Isn't that a bit aggravating?'

'Nice of you to care. Obviously, I'd prefer it if the club were making a profit. But there are two answers to your question. First, I suspect that you have a rather crude picture of the way businessmen like myself operate. We look successful, because looking successful is all part of being successful. But we don't have any magic formula. We don't always back winners. We throw a lot of bread upon the waters which simply goes soggy and gets eaten by seagulls. It's partly a question of knowing what to get into, partly a question of knowing when to get out, and partly a question of just pretending to know what you're doing.

'And the second thing is, I didn't buy this club because I wanted to make money. Of course, I'd prefer it if we roared up the table and were entertaining Juventus or Borussia Munchengladbach every other week, and building new stands et cetera. But if I'd been thinking return on capital, I wouldn't have sunk whatever it was into Athletic. I'm just nuts about the game, that's the fact of the matter. Ever meet a kid who didn't want to own a football club? Wildest dream.'

'Used to play the game, did you, Mr Prosser?'

'Wanted to. Wanted to. You may not believe this, but as a kid I was too fat. Too fat and too brainy.'

'I'm a goalkeeper,' said Duffy. Sometimes he thought he was prouder of being goalkeeper for the Reliables than of any other thing in his life. Well, perhaps that wasn't surprising: what would be number two source of pride?

'You look a little short for a goalkeeper,' said Mr Prosser. 'Also a bit – how shall I put it? – a bit stocky for a goalkeeper. Is that why you're on the Slimline?'

'So you're seven-figure rich and you're pouring money into Athletic …'

'Not pouring, Mr Duffy. A little dribble. And you've no idea how useful a loss can be here and there in the books.'

'And you've absolutely no enemies.'

'What a silly word that is.'

'Can we start at the beginning again, Mr Prosser?'

'Wherever you like. As long as you don't charge poor James for the petrol. The Corniche can be a little heavy on fuel, especially in London traffic.'

Duffy took a swig at his tonic water. Nasty crack, that, about the Slimline. He was just in training, that's all. In training twelve months of the year. In training for not getting fat.

'OK. So we have a football club. Third Division, slipping a bit. Slipping quite a bit. Deep down in the relegation zone. Scrambling for points. Gates dropping, not enough money coming through the turnstiles. New manager unable to stop the rot. Some hopeful signs, though, especially the way young Danny Matson is play-ing, and the understanding he's striking up with Brendan Domingo. Not out of the wood yet, not by a long way, but there's a little bit of light at the end of the tunnel, as the manager keeps saying.

'Then, what happens? The clever little midfielder who happens to be prompting the revival walks into a good kicking in an underground car-park. Rather a lot of them doing the kicking if they were only after thirty quid and a Barclaycard. They didn't even borrow his motor, either. They just made sure he wasn't going to be out playing one-twos for quite some time.

'Very unfortunate for the club, just when they were beginning to pull round a bit. Still, they say crisis brings out the best in everybody, so what happens next? Young Brendan Domingo starts taking more responsibility, the other lads chip in, and Danny Matson isn't missed that much. Is this a bit more light at the end of the tunnel? It might be, but someone comes up to Brendan in the Albion and suggests an early wage packet for seeing to it that Athletic gets relegated. In the nicest possible way, of course. Big Bren tells him where to shove it, and what happens? A few days later Bren gets fixed on a rather clever rape charge. It may not work out in the end, but it'll be enough to keep him out of the game until the end of the season, and perhaps for several seasons to come. No Danny, no Brendan, no Athletic.

'And just in case this isn't enough to do for the club, there's bits of agg off the pitch as well. Like a very nasty bunch of yobbos up one end, who all of a sudden start turning against one of their own team's star players. A very nasty bunch of yobbos organised by some neo-Nazi nutter funded by we know not who. Could be anyone. Plus which there's another bit of agg from a normally very quiet set of residents, who for some reason take it into their heads to sue the club and close the Layton Road end. Thereby ensuring that the yobbos get more chance of mixing with the away fans, and that the club has to pay out more money for more coppers, and that the average home fan thinks twice before taking his wife and kids down to the ground. How does it sound so far?'

'It's like listening to Jimmy Lister. Another Slimline?'

'No thanks.'

'Probably the wise decision. Well, it doesn't sound anything to me, Mr Duffy. It sounds less than anything. Are you suggesting that I ought to be more concerned than I am?'

'I don't know how concerned you are, Mr Prosser.'

'I'm very concerned about this club being relegated. But what are you telling me? That there've been two criminal acts relating to members of the playing staff over the last few weeks. Quite right there have, and they're both being looked into by the police with what is I am sure a proper diligence. Whether the criminal acts are as you described them, though, seems dubious to me. Matson was always a bit of a hothead, and he admitted he was drunk at the time; what more natural than for him to get into a fight? And how do we know there were these dozens of un-identifiable men descending on him? Perhaps there was only one. With Matson in the condition even he admits he was in, one would have been enough. It might have been a schoolgirl. Some schoolgirl in need of thirty quid for the hairdresser or something.

'As for Domingo, I'm sure he'd be touched by your loyalty, and I'm sure there are two sides to the story, but until it comes up in court it seems to me that we have to accept the police's view. I've always liked Domingo myself, both as a player and as a person. I don't know him that well, of course; though I know him a lot better than you do. And since we're hazarding reckless guesses, I'll give you my guess. Brendan had been booed rotten by the Layton Road end all Saturday afternoon. Then he'd got us the winning goal, and only the directors' box applauded. He's had this treatment for weeks – you may even have seen my note in the programme a couple of weeks ago deploring the loutish behaviour of certain untypical groups of so-called fans. He's always pretended it didn't affect him, but how much self-control can you have? So he's been made to feel unwelcome, to put it mildly, all afternoon, and then after the match which he's won for us he goes down the boozer, meets a girl who invites him back to her place, and just when he thinks the whole white world isn't against him after all, she suddenly turns unwelcoming as well; starts going on about a woman's right to choose, or whatever. He isn't the conquering hero after all, he's just a big black fellow who scores goals and then gets kicked around and jeered and turned down. So for once in a while he kicks back, his self-control snaps – and very unfortunate it is for all concerned.

'So what does that leave us with? The yobbos. Well, I'm sure you wouldn't say that yobbos are unique to this club. Or even the Red White and Blue Movement. I gather something similar happened down at Millwall, and I expect it happens elsewhere as well. We club chairmen are always trying to think up new strategies to combat hooliganism, I can give you my assurance on that one.

'The Layton Road residents? Well, I can't say I blame them, given the way some of our so-called fans behave. I'm surprised they've been so long-suffering. The other thing, the bribery? Deplorable, of course, but not un-usual. There's always a shortage of class players, and now there's a shortage of money as well. No club chairman is going to turn up his nose if some third party wants to earn himself a little drink.'

'So you're saying it's all coincidence?'

'I'm saying that when a club, or a business, or a

marriage, or anything is in trouble, then you'll always find that it never rains but it pours.'

Duffy grunted, and reached into his pocket.

'But what if there's someone up there making the clouds?'

'I wish I knew who it was who invented the phrase "conspiracy theory". It's been responsible for so much sloppy thinking.'

'Did you know her?'

'No. Should I? They're very good pictures. I didn't know you were a photographer, Duffy.'

'She's called Maggie Coleman. Or at least, she some-times is. She's the girl Brendan is supposed to have raped. But she's not always that. Sometimes she's called Denise. When she was called Denise she picked up Danny Matson at The Knight Spot, fought off the other girls through the evening, made sure he left with her, sent him off to the car-park alone while she waited at the club, and got him beaten up.'

'Is it really the same girl?'

'It's the same girl.'

'Well, she must like footballers.'

'Bit of a coincidence, isn't it?'

'Is it? There *are* girls who like footballers, you know, Duffy. I mean, I don't know if the outfit you play for is famous enough and, if I may say so, sexy enough to attract groupies, but it's no rare phenomenon in the Football League. Both Matson and Domingo are attrac-tive to women, I should imagine. I don't think we should disapprove of her morals just because she allowed herself to be taken home by both of them. Indeed, perhaps she should have our sympathy, given that neither of her romantic evenings with the stars of the local team went according to plan.'

'They didn't go to plan for Danny and Brendan either.'

'Then we must sympathise all round.'

'Don't you think it's a bit iffy that she had dark hair and was called Denise when she met Danny, and had blonde hair and was called Maggie when she met Brendan?'

'Duffy, I'm not responsible for this young woman's behaviour. Ask her hairdresser, ask her mother, ask her psychiatrist, ask ...'

'Whoever's paying her?'

'No. Ask the girl herself.'

'I'd love to. Except that I'd get locked up for doing so.' Duffy put his glass down and started on the harder bit. 'And then we have the question of the planning permission.'

'The planning permission? Oh, Magrudo's joke. What's that got to do with anything?'

'Can I spin you a line, Mr Prosser?'

'Go ahead.'

'I mean, you won't take offence, or anything?'

'I can't promise not to.'

'Fair enough. Well, let's try this line. You bought the club, what, two years ago? It was pretty run down, losing money, falling gates, hadn't won anything for years. Everyone thinks, Ah, here comes the saviour. Local hero. Pump money into the club. New blood. All that sort of stuff – I remember reading it at the time myself. What they got wrong was, you never intended to save the club. In fact, you intended the opposite. You aren't interested in football, though you're very good at going through the motions. You've got away with looking like a chairman trying to pull the club up by its bootstraps, but all the time you've been letting the plug out on it.'

'Really? And how've I been doing that?' The tone was mild, polite, interested. Melvyn Prosser didn't look at all ready to admit being the Boston Strangler.

'Well, you appointed Jimmy Lister for a start. Very good player, nice man, rotten manager. Had a good little Second Division outfit and what did he do with it: in a couple of years he nearly got it relegated. Then out of the game for a year. That's not called bad luck, that's called the whisper going round about Jimmy Lister. And it wasn't a comment on his morals – they weren't worrying about their physios' wives. I bet he wasn't even offered a non-League team in all that year. You picked him up because you thought he was good at getting clubs relegated. And you gave him his head with all that silly stuff about kicking balls into the crowd and Bunnies sitting on his knee or whatever it was, which is all very well if you're riding high and pretty pathetic if you aren't. But that sort of thing makes people expect more from a club, so if you let him get on with it and then the club doesn't do the business on the pitch, then the manager looks more of a berk and the club looks even sillier.'

'I didn't know I was such a deep thinker,' said Melvyn Prosser. He was smiling at Duffy and following attentively, just as if he was being told a wonderful story he'd never heard before.

'I'm not sure I'd put it that high,' said Duffy. 'But you do look ahead. I think when you first got into all this you had some idea of how it might turn out. How you might make it turn out. Most people who look at a football ground see just that. A bloody great place where they play football. Something that's always been there, and always will be, even if it's looking a bit tatty at the time. You don't knock down a football stadium any more than you knock down a church.'

'They're knocking down churches nowadays.'

'Well there you are. That's what you saw. It looked tatty, and you thought, if I bought that, I could make it into a wonderful bit of development. So you started running the club down. And the worse it got, the more dependent on you it became. You didn't mind paying the bills because if anyone came along and was at all interested in buying it they'd take one look at the books and see how much it was costing you and they'd run away. You bought this club and instead of giving it a blood transfusion you cut its throat.'

'James will be saddened to hear that the fellow whose wages he is paying has such a low opinion of his professional capacities.'

'I think we have about the same opinion of Jimmy Lister, you and I, Mr Prosser.'

'So what do I do next?'

'Well, next you get Magrudo to apply for outline planning permission for the site.'

'Even though I haven't seen him for years.'

'Even though you haven't seen him for years except that you forget to tell various people like the staff at Hess House Holdings that you haven't seen him for years.'

Melvyn Prosser chuckled. He actually chuckled.

'I'm sorry. I didn't realise I was on oath when I spoke to you.'

'Then you get the permission and are all set on that side of things. Except that Jimmy Lister isn't quite running down the club quickly enough. He's done his best, but you can't actually be sure of relegation. So you decide to hurry things along. With Danny, and Brendan, and the residents. I don't know about the Red White and Blue – that might even be a coincidence.'

'Suddenly you're admitting there is such a thing as coincidence?'

'Yes.'

'Well, all right.' Melvyn handed him back the photographs. 'And that's my wife, by the way,' he added sarcastically.

'Then I suppose – not knowing as much about the business as you do – but I suppose you then have some system worked out with Charlie Magrudo. He's the front man, you're the money man; you sell him the ground for peanuts, then buy it back from him. I don't know how these things work—'

'Evidently.'

'But perhaps you bung him some work for his construction company as a thank-you present. Give him the contract for the leisure centre or something. Nice little leg-up for a business which hasn't always enjoyed the best of fortune.'

'I see. Is that it?'

'Yes. More or less.'

'And how do you rate my chances of getting detailed planning permission?'

'I don't know.'

'And what sort of profit am I looking to make?'

'I don't know.'

'Oh dear, how disappointing. And what would you say if I told you that you're living in cloud-cuckoo-land?'

'I wouldn't believe you.'

There was a pause. They were somewhere north of

Camden Town; Duffy wasn't exactly sure where. He couldn't understand Melvyn Prosser at all.

'Can I have another Slimline?'

'Of course. Would you help yourself? I always try and do the first drink and then let guests help themselves.'

Duffy poured out his tonic water.

'Yes. Definitely too small for a goalkeeper, I'd say. Even though I know less about the game than you, as you've so carefully pointed out.'

'I'm quite a good goalkeeper, actually,' said Duffy. 'Why aren't you angry?'

'Angry? I don't get angry. Not in business. Not even outside business. It doesn't ... work, I find.'

'But I've just accused you of committing grievous bodily harm and conspiring to pervert the course of justice.'

'Yes, I was thinking about that. If only I'd had the partition down and Hobbs had been listening, I could have sued you for slander.'

'I've put everything in my wife's name,' said Duffy. 'Like Charlie Magrudo.'

'Really? How interesting. For some reason I'd always thought you were queer. I do apologise.' Melvyn Prosser touched a button on his armrest console and the glass partition descended.

'Hobbs, will you stop in about two hundred and fifty yards' time.'

'Yessir.'

The partition slid up again, and the Corniche came smoothly to a halt. 'If I let you out here, Mr Duffy, I think you'll find you're exactly halfway between two tube stations. I'm afraid I can't take you any further.'

'Thanks for the lift. See you at the game.'

Duffy got out on to a damp pavement somewhere

between Tufnell Park and Archway. Why did he almost like Melvyn Prosser? He should try and stop almost liking Melvyn Prosser. It was a funny feeling: you put the chisel into the wall and twist, and nothing happens. The chisel's intact; the wall hasn't shifted an inch; everything's the same.

'Cheers, mate,' said a passing figure.

Duffy realised that he was still holding a cut-glass tumbler containing half a Slimline tonic.

Duffy woke up, and went through his ritual lymph-node check. Groin, armpits, neck. All the usual little bumps and knobs, as far as he could see, but nothing actually in raging motion. Night sweats? Erections? No, the score was still the same. Erections 2, Night Sweats 2, after extra time and several replays. No doubt Binyon could have explained it all to Duffy. 'You get the night sweats, Duffy, because you've got AIDS, and you've got AIDS because you're queer. The erections are merely a hysterical reaction designed to convince yourself that you might after all be straight, or at least – what's that quaint expression of yours? – bisexual; that's it. Your sweats are telling you the truth, your dick is lying.' Something like that.

The trouble was, if Binyon were sitting on the next barstool at the Alligator, Duffy would have been inclined to believe him. But at the moment he only had himself to do the explaining. So, with the full bravery acquired by one who has successfully got through a whole night on his tod, Duffy decided that he had got the night sweats – only two, after all – because he was really worried about something. What he was really worried about was getting night sweats. Nothing unusual in this; it was rather like having a hysterical pregnancy. Not that Duffy had

had one of those … And as for the erections, well, he thought, let's take the simplest course. You had an erection in bed with Carol because you fancied her: there's nothing complicated about that, is there? So why hadn't he had one the last two nights she'd stayed? Well, the second night we were a bit distant with one another because I'd bullied her into looking those names up on the computer for me; and the first night … The first night? I don't know, maybe I had a headache or something. Oh yes? Go tell that one to Binyon.

The evening before, Athletic had lost two–nil to Wigan. Duffy had watched the game from the Layton Road end, where the yobbos still congregated after kicking their way through all the other fans, and there was little to take heart from. It wasn't a case of the mid-table club being more relaxed because they didn't have any promotion or relegation worries, and fretful Athletic being over-anxious. It was just a case of one team being better than the other: quicker, cleverer, more willing to contest the ball in midfield, and sharper in finishing. 'No excuses,' Jimmy Lister told the *Chronicle*, 'they were the better side on the night.'

'Is it back to the drawing board, Jimmy?' asked Ken Marriott (the real Ken Marriott).

'No, it's not back to the drawing board. No one's going to give us a new set of pencils at this stage of the season. We're not going to panic. It's just a question of battling away. The lads know what they have to do, and they know that the chairman and the management are right behind them.'

The lads knew what they had to do: they had to win every game. They also had to hope that the other teams immediately above them would continue to drop points.

And short of sending hit squads round the country to maim half a dozen fiery little midfield schemers and frame half a dozen skilful black strikers, there was no certain method of making that happen.

Ken Marriott had also had a brief interview with the chairman of Athletic. Yes, he was right behind the lads who were battling away but just not getting the breaks. No, he hadn't given up hope of Third Division football at the Athletic ground next season. Well, he didn't want to talk about the other possibility because he didn't want to put the lads under any more pressure than they were; but everyone knew that the club was making a considerable loss, and that while the chairman was happy to sustain that loss until the end of the season, he'd obviously have to reconsider his own position, and indeed the club's whole future, if Athletic were relegated.

Well, that was clear enough, thought Duffy. It was also a bit clever: while claiming he didn't want to put the lads under any more pressure, Prosser was doing just that: saying that he'd pull the plug on them if they went down. And he would, too: this was the first time he'd gone into print on the subject, and Duffy was sure he meant more than every word. Melvyn Prosser would slit the club's throat.

And what could Duffy do about it? Nothing, unless he could get the team playing again. After all, if Athletic somehow managed to stay in the Third Division, that would be a considerable embarrassment to Prosser. He might sack Jimmy Lister – though that probably wouldn't get him anywhere if he'd chosen Jimmy in the first place because he thought he wasn't any good; replace Lister and the club might find itself with a real manager who'd push them to a safe place in mid-table. But how could Duffy get the team playing? He couldn't exactly mend Danny Matson's leg with superglue, or dynamite Brendan Domingo out of his cell.

He could try and stir things up a little, though.

'Maggot?'

'Yeah.'

'Ready for the game on Sunday? Honing the vision?'

'Sometimes I think you're taking the piss, Duffy. Actually, I'm more worried about Saturday's fixture. If they lose again, anything could happen.'

'Yeah. Tell me, Maggot, me being only a cub reporter and all that, tell me, would it be a story,' Duffy tried to sound as if he really wasn't sure, 'if there were plans to knock down the Athletic ground and build a shopping centre all over the top of it?'

'I think it'd be a sensation. Are you taking the piss again?'

'Promise not. I've done a little work on it myself' – he heard Maggot groan – 'No, not like last time. I mean, I was me, and I wasn't from the *Chronicle*.'

Duffy explained about the outline planning permission. Well, if Prosser and Magrudo had both been assuring him it was just a little joke so that Charlie could think about Mel's face when he opened the papers, why not give them both the thrill? Duffy acted the cub reporter a bit with Ken Marriott, but wasn't short of advice. He mustn't fail to point out that Prosser and Magrudo were old friends and business associates, and that staff at Hess House Holdings had confirmed to a reporter that the two men had been having a lot of meetings lately. Duffy wondered if Maggot would hint that Melvyn Prosser had been an old friend of Mrs Charlie Magrudo. He didn't think the *Chronicle* would stretch that far, but he threw it in anyway. He warned Marriott that both the chairman of Athletic and the managing director of Magrudo Construction would claim that it was all a joke. Duffy even had the temerity to suggest that Maggot could take some line about whether the Athletic players and the Athletic fans would see the humour of the situation, given the club's current plight.

The story appeared on the Friday, ATHLETIC GROUND FOR REDEVELOPMENT? ran the headline on the inside-page splash. ITALIAN STYLE PIAZZA LOOK it said underneath, which Duffy liked, as it would bring out the patriotism of the fans; and underneath that, in smaller capitals but still prominent: CHAIRMAN DENIES CLUB TO FOLD. Ken Marriott had done the job well: Prosser and Magrudo's suggestion that the whole thing was 'a joke' was slipped in just at the right moment, making them seem to be either outright liars or at best people with a very sinister sense of humour.

On the Saturday, Athletic were at home to Bristol Rovers, and as Melvyn Prosser took his seat the main stand booed him. Duffy, from the Piggeries terrace, had a quiet smile. On the other hand, it wasn't that funny: it meant that the only well-behaved part of the home crowd was now joining in the fun of turning on the club in some way. The yobs would have booed Brendan if he'd been there; but he wasn't, so instead the season-ticket holders booed the chairman. To any outsider it would seem that the whole place was falling apart, and it didn't seem to do the home team's confidence much good. Bristol Rovers unstitched them comprehensively in midfield, fooled them with a free-kick ploy just before half-time, and never looked like losing. One–nil, Athletic second from bottom, and though he'd been booed, Melvyn Prosser might well have found it a rewarding day in the stands. Duffy didn't know whether he'd come out ahead on his ploy with the *Chronicle*, or further behind.

On Sunday morning there was a ring at his door. Duffy felt nervous. No one had tried to beat him up yet. No one had tried to frame him for rape. Prosser would have known that Duffy had been behind the *Chronicle* story. Perhaps he'd sent round some heavies. The doorbell rang again.

'Who is it?'

There was a loud bellow from outside in an American accent.

'Open the door, schmuck, or I'll break it down with this pickaxe.'

Phew. That was a relief, thought Duffy, and opened the door immediately.

'You had me worried, just ringing the bell like that. Come in.'

Geoff Bell wandered in and started looking around Duffy's flat as if he expected it to be bugged.

'Like the way you keep this place, Duffy. Not too much stuff around. Bit of a challenge to plant something on you.'

'Well, you know, Geoff, I like to think of all eventualities.'

'Mind you, that door of yours is chronic. No one in his right mind has a door like that. I mean, you might as well just leave it wide open when you go out.'

'I'll look into it. I promise. Social call?'

Geoff Bell never made social calls, as Duffy well knew. Quite what Geoff Bell did for a social life – apart, that is, from turn out in home matches for the Reliables every other Sunday – was a mystery to Duffy. One day he'd ask Geoff, though Geoff might well not understand the question.

'Thought you might like to see these.'

There were about two dozen large black-and-white photographs, and Duffy almost didn't glance at them, since he knew he'd have to sit through a lengthy explanation of lighting conditions, lenses, depth of field and film-speed first. But the top picture immediately caught his attention. It showed Maggie Coleman, or was it Denise given that she had dark hair again, leaning back against a wall with her shoulders and pushing her hips out towards a man in a mackintosh whose cheek she was stroking. It appeared to be raining, but Maggie's own raincoat was unbuttoned at the front, and her skirt was very short.

While Geoff droned on about the difficulties of choosing film-speed when using a 200mm lens in poor light, Duffy shuffled slowly through the photographs. You didn't need to be a copper who'd once done three years in Soho to know that Maggie Coleman was more than just an average friendly girl with a striking sense of fashion. There were photos of Maggie getting in and out of cars (Geoff had usefully included the number plates in one or two of the shots), Maggie accosting, Maggie raising the middle finger and shouting at some punter who'd probably said she wasn't worth *that* much. Back at work so soon after a broken nose? Maggie Coleman must have a lot of grey-haired old mothers to support, or a very gabby pimp. On the other hand, it wasn't so surprising. Maggie wouldn't need her nose to ply her trade. Whores don't kiss.

'Where were these taken, Geoff?'

'On the back.'

Times, dates, places, all written neatly.

'You see I wasn't really happy with that first set I did for you. I could tell you weren't happy either, Duffy. Wanted to know whether they were good likenesses or something, I seem to remember you saying. Well, these are good likenesses.'

Duffy wasn't sure whether Bell was teasing or not. Knowing him, quite possibly not.

'Would it be possible to run me off another set, Geoff? I know we're playing at twelve.'

'*You're* playing at twelve.'

'Sorry.' Duffy should have remembered that Geoff still believed he ought to be included for away matches as well. Not for his skill in surveillance, but for his skill on the pitch.

'Well, I thought you might ask,' said Geoff, producing another large brown envelope.

'You're brilliant, Geoff, do you know that? You could probably tell me what I'm thinking.'

'You're thinking, I wonder if he really does care about being left out of away games. And the answer is yes I bloody do. I'm just as good defensively as Maggot, and I don't have half so many potty ideas as he does.'

'Quite wrong, Geoff. I was wondering how much Maggie Coleman charged.'

'Liar.'

'You're brilliant, Geoff.'

'Yeah.'

As Duffy drove to the game, he thought about the photographs. Of course they weren't conclusive. Nothing in this whole business had ever been conclusive. But they were something extra. They certainly threw a little doubt on Melvyn Prosser's theory that Maggie Coleman was just a nice girl who liked footballers – unless, that is, all the gentlemen in Geoff Bell's photos were footballers. Sure, thought Duffy, the whole of the First Division out on a coach trip.

Of course, just because Maggie and Denise Coleman were two girls of distinctly flexible morals didn't mean that the coppers would throw out the charges against Brendan. Judges and coppers no longer assumed that all women secretly wanted to be raped, that girl hitchhikers deserved everything they got, and that whores were outside the protection of the law. Whores got raped, just as housewives got raped: even the coppers were beginning to acknowledge that. On the other hand, this didn't make the coppers feel that whores were deeply misunderstood girls with nice honest natures; it didn't make the coppers step in when a girl was arguing prices with a punter and say, 'No, she's worth more than that – more than she's asking, in fact. Go on, Maggie, put your prices up, you're something special.' No, the coppers wouldn't be doing that for a while yet.

What they might do, if they saw these photographs, was have a much closer look at Maggie Coleman's evidence. And what they might do, if they also were in possession of a statement from Danny Matson that Maggie was also Denise, was have a much closer look at her motives, her background, and her business associates. They might put the Matson case and the Domingo case together and start digging – and do it with a few more resources than Duffy had at his disposal. And if Jimmy Lister's solicitor was smart, and if he made the right noises about possible conspiracy but didn't make them too loudly, and if they weighed in with Brendan's blameless past, and if the police solicitors could be persuaded to drop their objection to bail, then the magistrates might just be persuaded to open the slammer next Wednesday and let Brendan out into the sunlight. Bail for rape was a tricky decision, but if the magistrates could shift their responsibility on to the police solicitors, it could just be swung. Whether that would make any difference, Duffy didn't know. Would Jimmy Lister dare play the lad? And in any case, what would Brendan's fitness be like after ten days walking up and down a little cell?

The Reliables played well that Sunday, and were unlucky to lose by the only goal of the game: Maggot's vision induced him to square-pass across his own penalty area, and then, when the pass was intercepted, to bring down the opponent with a rugby tackle. The penalty was whacked past Duffy, who didn't feel too bad about it: keepers are never blamed for penalties. They may be made to look silly, but they aren't blamed.

On Sunday evening Carol came round and they had pizzas again.

'I like the way you've done the peppers,' she said. 'You've arranged them just exactly the way you did last time. Did you realise that, Duffy?'

Duffy grunted.

'Only if I could make a very tiny criticism this time, they're not as crisp as they ought to be. They're a bit soggy.'

Duffy grunted again. It was just that he didn't like sleeping with half a pizza in his bed. Couldn't anyone understand that? For Christ sake, what did other people do? Move the fridge into the bedroom and throw a few packets of frozen peas in between the sheets, just for company?

'Mine's all right,' said Duffy.

'Delicious,' muttered Carol. Why had he done the crust like that? Another thing added to the list of what she couldn't ask him about.

She'd had a quiet Sunday at West Central; quiet enough to check out the names Duffy had asked her about. Not much help, she was afraid. Melvyn Prosser and Charlie Magrudo were clean. Maggie Coleman had one charge of soliciting, about a year ago, in Shepherd's Market. Come down in the world since, thought Duffy. Oh well, every little helps; the coppers wouldn't object to being reminded of that.

On the Monday Duffy went down to the Athletic ground, keeping a sharp eye out for gold Corniches which looked as if they might want to run over his foot, and showed Jimmy Lister the dossier on Maggie Coleman. Then he bullied him. He had to bully him quite a lot. Jimmy Lister was wary of the coppers, and wary of solicitors, and Duffy had to remind him quite hard that as the club was paying the solicitor's bill, the club had a say in what the solicitor did.

'OK, OK, I'll do it,' said Jimmy eventually. 'But playing the lad is another matter.'

'You don't think he'll be fit?'

'No, I shouldn't think he'll have lost much being locked up. Sometimes a lay-off at this stage of the season actually sharpens them up.'

'Well, there you are.'

'But would it be fair on the lad? I mean, would it be fair? Just think what a roasting they'd give the lad from the terraces.'

'They give him a roasting anyway. He gets booed every time he touches the ball here. He gets booed away from home. What's the difference?'

'They can be very nasty, you know, the fans.'

'What do you think Brendan will want to do?'

'He'll want to play, of course he will.'

'Then let him. It's his career.'

'Yes, but as manager I've got to look after the boy. I've got to think about his long-term interests.'

'What about everyone's long-term interests?' asked Duffy.

'How do you mean?'

'I don't think you've got a choice. You're getting relegated at the moment, no doubt about it. You need all the points you can get. Nine from the last three matches and you could well be safe. Six and there's an outside chance. Three or less and you're sunk. Fourth Division and a salary drop for all the lads; that is, if the whole place doesn't get concreted over first. Slow plane to Abu Dhabi for Jimmy Lister, except that the Abu Dhabi offer somehow doesn't seem to be coming through. And if you do drop, not that it will then be a matter of concern to you, the club loses Brendan. Some Second Division outfit is sure to snap him up. Play him and you might just have a chance of staying up – and keeping Brendan. Don't play him and you lose him, and maybe everything else as well: the team, the job, the ground.'

'Put like that, Duffy …'

'Yes?'

'But I'm still worried about the fans. They can say the cruellest things, you know, Duffy. Things you wouldn't imagine they could think up.'

'Earplugs,' said Duffy sharply. 'Earplugs.'

While Jimmy Lister went off to see the coppers, Duffy drove off to the group of five streets whose names were on the back of Geoff Bell's photographs. The lunchtime trade on a Monday was always a bit slack – punters were slow recuperating from the weekend – so there was a fair chance he might find her. As he slowed the car and started a bit of furtive eyes-left, he wondered what the going rate was nowadays for impersonating a police officer. Or for blackmail.

He lowered the passenger window in preparation. Then up and down, round the square, eyes half on the road, half squirting off in search of those gaudy, lounging figures who pecked at the pavement with their high heels. Up and down again, round the square: no wonder the residents objected. It wasn't just that respectable women got propositioned by thick punters; it was having to bring up your children in an atmosphere of pure exhaust fumes. Now, once more, and, and, what about ... *There* she is.

'You doing business?' It was probably the least necessary question Duffy had ever asked; but he said it routinely, as if establishing his credentials. Maggie – or perhaps Denise as she still had dark hair – was already checking the car: inspecting the back to see that there wasn't a second punter lurking on the floor, checking the driver to see that he wasn't an obvious psycho.

'Twenty-five,' she said. This wasn't the smartest end of town. What would she have been pulling down in Shepherd's Market? Four times that? Six times? Ten times, perhaps; especially if she landed an Arab. Maggie Coleman had come down in the world.

'Hop in, darling.'

She got in quickly, filling the car with a scent like air freshener. Perhaps it was air freshener, given some of the punters she'd have to consort with at her current going rate. She put her hand on Duffy's thigh and said, 'Twyford Avenue, you know it? Money first.'

'Course, darling,' said Duffy. 'What's yer name?'

'Sharron.'

Duffy waited until he had got up enough speed for it to be inadvisable to jump out, then murmured, 'Well, Sharron, I shall call you Denise if that's all right.'

'Whatever you like.'

'Or maybe I shall call you Maggie.'

'Call me the Queen of Sheba if that's your thing.'

'And you can call me Detective-Sergeant Hawkins, C Division.'

She reacted to that, at least.

'You shit, you fucker, you pulling me in for that? Copper. Fucking *copper*. You'd think I could smell fucking copper by now, wouldn't you?' Duffy gave a little smile. 'You pulling me in for that? You fucking came up and *asked*, copper. It's not soliciting if a copper comes past with his truncheon hanging out of the window.'

'Well, maybe I'm not pulling you in, Maggie.'

'I see. You want a bit of free, too? Listen, I give out so much free to you coppers I might as well come down the station one day and do it there. Save breaking up my working day, wouldn't it?'

'That's not a bad plan.'

'Listen, I've got this baby girl ...'

'Shove it.' Duffy stopped the car. 'Do you know who lives over there?'

'Course I don't, copper.'

'Danny Matson.'

'Who?'

'He sits in his chair all day with his foot up on a stool.'

'What, does he need a girl or something? You treating him?'

'He'd be very pleased to see you.'

'It's thirty for, you know, cripples and so on.' Duffy usually quite liked whores. This one he found less appealing.

'You set up Danny Matson, you framed Brendan Domingo. Who paid?'

'Friends of yours, are they? Never heard of them meself.'

'Who paid?'

'What do you mean? Punters pay. Only coppers get it for free, copper.'

'Danny's out of the game for life, Brendan's facing five years, now who paid?' Duffy was squeezing the driving wheel hard; afraid that otherwise he might be squeezing something else instead. Somebody's windpipe, for instance.

Silence.

'Was it Prosser? Was it? Was it Magrudo?'

Silence.

'OK, I'll just have to throw the book at you, Maggie.'

'There's not much in your book, copper.'

'Soliciting, GBH, attempting to pervert the course of justice.'

'Don't make me laugh.'

'Well, we'll see who the jury believes – you or Brendan. It's five years for one or the other of you.'

'You're just a dry wank, copper. You can't scare me. Who would a jury believe, a tart or a nignog? They'd just tell us to bugger off and not make so much noise next time we're screwing.'

She wasn't stupid; that was a pity. She wasn't stupid,

and she didn't scare. Duffy tried to think of another line of attack. He failed. She didn't.

'But I'd plead guilty to the soliciting. I'd do that. And I'd throw myself on the court's mercy and say I was terribly, terribly sorry and that it would never happen again and was there anything they could do to stop the boys in blue asking for so much free?'

'Get out, Maggie.'

'You're a dry wank, copper, you know that? A dry wank.'

'Cheers,' said Brendan Domingo when the police released him and explained the terms of his bail. 'Cheers,' said Brendan Domingo when Jimmy Lister said he'd risk him in the first game, see how it went, and then make a decision about the last two. 'Cheers,' said Brendan Domingo when Duffy explained his idea about the earplugs.

At home to Newport, away to Hull, at home to Preston. Win all three and they'd have a real chance of escaping relegation. Lose more than one and they were for the drop. Something in between and it all depended on how their fellow-strugglers got on.

Duffy stood on the Layton Road terrace for the Newport game, and the yobbos were not well behaved. They may not have had the full powers of concentration when it came to spelling, but they could all certainly read. Read the headlines in the local paper, at least. 'OH, NAUGHTY-NAUGHTY, NAUGHTY-NAUGHTY-NAUGHTY-NAUGHTY BRE-HEN-DAN' was one of their politer chants. Others were more specific; they turned on Brendan's colour, and the African jungle, and the function of his middle leg. Every time Brendan touched the ball, several hundred yobbos booed, and several hundred yobbos' fists went up in the air and made wanking gestures.

Brendan, his ears blocked, didn't notice. Duffy was more worried about the effect the noises might have on the rest of the Athletic side; but they appeared not to notice either. Having Brendan back seemed to relax them; and for a change, the opposition clearly had their minds on their summer holidays. After forty minutes Athletic won a free kick on the edge of the Newport area. Brendan took a long run and smashed it straight at the wall. It took a deflection off a defender's shoulder, lobbed into the air, spun across the goal area with a deceiving bounce, and was sliced off a Newport defender's boot into an Athletic chest, from where it cannoned unstoppably past the keeper. A real end-of-season goal; one–nil; three points.

'I think we can do it, Duffy,' said Jimmy Lister after the match. 'I really think we can do it.'

'How's Brendan taking things?'

'Oh, a bit subdued, you know. Just thinking about his game, I suppose.'

'What did the police say?'

'They said, Score a hat-trick and we'll drop the charges. Funny sense of humour, I thought.'

'Yes, well, they're like that.' They were; Duffy remembered some of the things that seemed funny to coppers. 'Two more wins, then, Jimmy?'

'On my granny's life, I promise you.'

However, both of Jimmy Lister's grandmothers had been dead some time, and the midweek away game at Hull confirmed it. Two–nil down at half-time, three–nil down after fifty minutes. Jimmy pulled off a midfielder and put on a wide man; Brendan took out his earplugs and threw them at the bench; but neither move made any difference. The Athletic midfield was underpopulated; the wide man didn't get a kick; and Hull walked in another goal. 'We were beaten by the better side on the day,' Jimmy told the *Chronicle*. 'But the season's never over until the final whistle's been blown.'

Events the next day in the north of England unexpectedly made things easier for Athletic; or if not easier, at least clearer. Port Vale finished their season with a handy defeat leaving them still only two points above Athletic. So if Athletic lost or drew their final match, they'd be relegated; if they won, by however fine a margin, they stayed up. 'The lads know exactly what they have to do,' said Jimmy Lister. 'It's all down to us now.'

On the morning of the Preston match, Duffy got Carol to have another look at his back.

'It's still there, Duffy, like it was last time I looked.'

'Thanks.'

In the bathroom, before he shaved, he did his lymph-node check. No movement on that front. No blotches on his legs either. No more night sweats. How long before he could count on being safe? Six months? A year?

When he came back from the bathroom he was whistling. Carol smiled at him. She wondered why he kept wanting her to check his back. She wondered why the pizza he'd cooked her the night before had been even soggier than the previous one. Were the two eccentricities connected? Did he think crisp pizzas brought you out in a rash? He was an odd one and no mistake. Always worrying about something. Always on the move. Why couldn't they sometimes have a nice lie-in, like other people?

'Duffy, one of these days, will you bring me breakfast in bed?'

A puzzled look came over Duffy's face, followed by one of horror as he thought of toast-crumbs in the sheets.

'Of course not,' he said. 'Never.'

'Oh well. I suppose not. What about in a hotel?'

'What d'you mean?'

'Have you ever had room service in a hotel, Duffy?'

'Of course not.' What a ridiculous idea.

'Neither have I.'

Duffy was puzzled. He didn't know what Carol was going on about. Perhaps she wanted something.

'Do you want to come down the match with me?'

'What, the Reliables?' Carol was usually forbidden from watching Duffy play; it made him nervous, he claimed.

'No, the Athletic. Against Preston.'

'The Athletic? Against Preston? Of course not. I've got some standards, Duffy.'

'Uh-huh.' That can't have been what she wanted, then.

On his way to the ground, Duffy took a short diversion and knocked at number 37 Layton Road.

'Mr Bullivant.'

'Ah, it's the laddy with the big pencil and the small brain.'

'Mr Bullivant, I wonder if I could have a quote from you about the proposed redevelopment of the Athletic ground?'

'Now why ever should you want a thing like that? Can't you use one of those other remarks of mine I remember you copying down into your book?'

'But are the residents happy about the proposed scheme?'

'This particular resident doesn't give a tinker's, sonny.'

'Why's that?'

'Because by next season I shall be able to go for a short

walk from my home and watch a class outfit by the name of Tottenham Hotspur.'

'You're moving? You're selling your house?'

Mr Bullivant winked. 'Sold it two months ago, laddy.' And then he shut the door.

The Preston match was never going to be easy. Duffy knew what he wanted – a three–nil win with Brendan scoring a hat-trick – and he knew what little chance there was of getting it. Besides, the Preston management had just announced that its first-team squad would have to be reduced next year. Every place was up for grabs; it was going to be musical chairs with five seats short instead of just the one.

The crowd was bigger than it had been for the last ten home games. The twin possibilities of relegation and redevelopment had brought an extra two hundred through the turnstiles. Two hundred ghouls, keen to witness a death.

The Piggeries end were in good voice, but the rest of the crowd was subdued. A hot spring sun made the football seem unreal, and time went quickly. Two corners, a free kick and a couple of throw-ins, it seemed, and the referee was already blowing his whistle for half-time. Nil–nil. No good at all to Athletic. No sign, either, of what they could do about it. Brendan had been a bit subdued; neat, but subdued. Duffy wondered what Melvyn Prosser was thinking. Forty-five minutes from … from what? From the sound of Charlie Magrudo's bulldozers?

Athletic were playing towards the Layton Road end in the second half; though most of the action was taking place in the clogged midfield. Slowly, it seemed, Preston were beginning to batten Athletic down. They won a couple of free kicks in dangerous positions, and then a corner. Everyone went deep into the Athletic half except for Brendan, the big Preston centre-back, and the Preston keeper. The corner was an outswinger, the Athletic keeper committed himself too early, and was dragged further and further out of his goal in pursuit of the ball. To everyone's relief he caught it, somewhere near the penalty spot. Three strides and he was at the edge of his area and giving the ball a hoofing drop kick. Chase that one, you buggers, he seemed to say, and eighteen players did. Two, however, had a good thirty yards start on them. Or rather, suddenly, just one: Brendan. The big Preston defender had tripped, somehow – did anyone see what happened? – and was lying on his back near the centre-circle. Brendan was sprinting alone towards the Preston goal, his head cocked as he watched the ball descend towards him. The keeper, seeing his centre-back on the ground, came out fast. Bring him down, Duffy found himself whispering; and he was talking to the keeper, not Brendan. Both players went up in a flail of arms; both players came down in a flail of legs; the ball, quietly, bounced over their falling bodies and continued its unimpeded progress until it settled in the back of the Preston net. One–nil.

No one knew where to run. Half the Athletic team ran to their keeper; half to Brendan. Most of the Preston team besieged the referee, claiming offside, a foul on the centre-back or a foul on the goalkeeper, according to their temperament. A few went over to the linesman and expressed doubts about his eyesight, parentage and sexual habits when alone. A couple bent over the prostrate keeper, who was feigning injury quite well and worrying about next season's first-team squad. One–nil.

Preston, not surprisingly, seemed to resent the goal,

and attacked with an additional muscularity. Brendan, for his part, found himself on the end of some close attention from the big centre-back who had earlier mysteriously lost his footing. There would be bruises to count on the Sunday morning. But Athletic weren't eager to throw away their sudden gift. They scrambled, they hoofed, they scrapped, they battled; they were not above getting a touch physical themselves; and their keeper, spurred on by his first goal ever in League football, saved them twice with full-length sprawls. Suddenly, it was all over. One–nil. Athletic were safe.

Ten members of the Athletic team ran towards Jimmy Lister's dug-out. There was hugging and shouting, and a few tears were shed, before they all turned to the main stand for acclaim. But the attention of the main stand was temporarily elsewhere. They were watching Brendan Domingo. So was Duffy, and he was a lot closer.

When the final whistle blew, Brendan had stopped where he was. He offered his hand to the Preston centre-back, who refused it, and carefully took out his earplugs. Then he began trotting very deliberately towards the Layton Road end. On his way he passed the Preston keeper and offered his hand, and was refused again. Slowly, he walked round behind the net until he faced the phalanx of yobbos. Duffy wondered what Brendan was going to do next, but he clearly had it all planned out. He began clapping the yobbos, as if thanking them for their kind advice in telling him to go back to the jungle. The yobbos were puzzled by this; but they were less puzzled by Brendan's next gesture. He turned his back to the Layton Road end, bent and lowered his shorts. The two white straps of his jock seemed to emphasise the blackness of his bum. He stayed like this for some five seconds, then pulled up his shorts, turned round, and started clapping the Layton Road enders again. Slowly, tauntingly. Duffy thought Brendan was extremely brave, even if there were a few coppers around.

Then, suddenly, Brendan was felled. He clutched the top of his head and keeled over heavily. The coppers, who had been looking on almost as puzzled as the yobbos, took this as their cue and waded into the terracing. The rest of the Athletic team, who had only caught the end of Brendan's performance, were already rushing over. The fans in the main stand started booing the yobbos at the Layton Road end. Must have been a coin, or a brick or something. The physio came running across and bent over Brendan. The police were vigorously bidding an end-of-season farewell to the yobbos. The main stand carried on booing, until, after a couple of minutes, Brendan got slowly to his feet; then they started cheering. While Jimmy Lister and the ten other players began a lap of honour, Brendan, his arm round the physio's shoulder, made his way groggily to the tunnel. Everyone knew ex-actly what had happened. Everyone except Duffy, that is.

An hour or so later he stood in the Athletic boardroom clutching a Slimline tonic and wondering whether he ought to be there. But Jimmy Lister had insisted. 'Might be the last time I can invite you up. Next year, who knows? Abu Dhabi?' It was clear to both of them that Abu Dhabi was a euphemism for the scrap-heap. Jimmy Lister hadn't yet established whether the Board was going to treat him as a hero for saving the club from relegation, or as a vil-lain for having got them into trouble. Duffy didn't think this was the moment to float his private theory about why Melvyn Prosser had hired Jimmy Lister in the first place.

He had three conversations as he sipped his Slimline.

Two of them were of professional interest, and related closely to the events of the last few weeks; and yet it was the third which intrigued him the most, and which he later wanted to tell Carol about.

The first conversation was with Ken Marriott, who was as surprised to see Duffy there as Duffy was to see him. Maggot told him, in an undertone, that soon after his article about the possible redevelopment of the ground had appeared, a number of long-time club supporters had founded a Reform Group.

'Not much chance of reforming things around here, is there?' said Duffy.

'Well, you can't be sure. The embarrassment factor is always worth something. And I'll be giving them quite a few inches on the sports pages. Better than nothing.'

'Sure.'

Duffy wasn't quite so sure after his second conversation. A hand took him suddenly by the elbow and turned him through 180 degrees. Melvyn Prosser. What's more, Melvyn Prosser smiling.

'Good to see you, Duffy. Make free with the Slimline. Didn't the lads do well?'

'Very well, Mr Prosser.'

'Can't thank you enough for getting Brendan out when you did. Without him I do declare we'd be in that place which we aren't allowed to mention inside this club.' Meaning the Fourth Division.

'I expect so.'

'You saved us, Duffy. I have to give you that. Maybe we should keep you on the payroll.'

'I'm not on it.'

'No, so you aren't. Well, come over here anyway, there's someone I'd like you to meet.' Prosser led Duffy across the boardroom towards a chunky, dark-suited man who had his back to them. Prosser elbowed him in the side to attract his attention.

'Duffy, I'd like you to meet my business partner, Charlie Magrudo. Charlie, this is Duffy, I was telling you about. We're thinking of putting Charlie on the Board.'

'Oh, yes,' said Duffy. 'Congratulations.'

'Haven't we met before?' asked Charlie, shaking him by the hand.

'I've got a brother,' said Duffy, 'I've got to go.'

What was all that about, he wondered. Was it a sneer? Was it a show of strength? Was it saying, You don't understand me, Duffy, and you never will? Was it saying, Fuck you, Duffy? He really didn't know. He wished Melvyn Prosser weren't almost likeable. For a villain, he nearly had a sense of fun.

'Hey, Duffy.'

'Brendan. How you doing?'

'Fine, terrific, never better. Thanks for the earplugs tip.'

'Thanks for the floor-show.'

'Yeah, well, I kind of lost me rag.'

'That's probably what most people would have thought.'

Brendan looked at him carefully.

'Meaning?'

Duffy smiled. 'Nice party, isn't it?'

'No, meaning? *Meaning?*' Brendan put a big, friendly arm round Duffy's shoulder and squeezed. Brendan was a lot bigger than Duffy.

'Meaning, well, I was standing pretty close to the yobbos, and I was watching you, and I didn't see anyone throw anything.'

'Duffy, didn't you see the way I went down? I was poleaxed.'

'Yes, I saw you go down, Brendan. I saw you go down like a striker in the box. The other thing I saw was that a club can hardly expect a player to abide by the terms of his contract with however many years left to run if he's just been felled by his own fans.'

Brendan's arm tightened round Duffy's shoulder.

'You know, man, you're a pretty clever fellow.'

'So are you.'

Brendan gave a deep chuckle.

'One of these days I might take you down The Palm Tree. Only trouble is, you're a bit scruffy.'

'One of these days I might come with you. Only trouble is, I'd steal all your girls.'

Duffy wondered why that made Brendan laugh so much.

'I expect because he thought you were one of the other sort,' said Carol when he related the conversation to her.

'The what? Oh. Uh.' Everyone seemed to think he was the other sort. Brendan thought so. Melvyn Prosser thought so. Binyon thought so. 'Do you think I am?'

'I don't know, Duffy. I don't really think about it much,' she said, lying.

'No, I don't think about it much either,' he said, telling the truth.

'Well in that case ...'

'Yes ...'

'We'd better do the washing up, hadn't we, Duffy?'

'Of course.'

'I thought you might say that.'

So they washed up, and then they put the things away, and then they wiped the draining board and the kitchen table, and then Duffy put the catch down on the front door, and then they went to the bathroom one after the other, and then they got into bed and turned out the light, and then Carol felt Duffy probing surreptitiously in his armpits for his lymph nodes, and then they both tried to go to sleep. This is what being married for a very long time must feel like, thought Carol.

And then Duffy got an erection. At first Carol thought it might be his hand that was moving, looking for another lymph node somewhere. But they were lying like spoons so closely that there wasn't room for a hand. She tried to breathe very gently, and listen to see if he was awake. Did she want him to be awake or not? She didn't really know. That other time, she couldn't be sure she hadn't imagined it. But this time, this time ... She tried not to breathe at all, so that she could listen to Duffy's breathing. It wasn't giving anything away. Oh, this was just silly.

'Duffy,' she said quietly, 'Duffy, am I awake?'

He stirred slightly.

'You're awake,' he said finally, 'I'm dreaming.'

Extra Time

Extra Time

The first ten minutes of the second half were a bit lively. Both sides were deliberately playing it tight, and both had a victim marked for special attention. After two minutes Maggot, who had been looking a little jumpy since the whistle went, surrendered to his wilder instincts and tried to sandbag one of the pub team's midfield. Oooff, went Duffy, as the midfielder seemed to forget about the ball and just drove through Maggot, one knee right on line for the wedding tackle. Oooff. Then, a minute or so later, in clear retribution, the speedy little ginge was slowed down by a well-contrived sandwich between Barney – bit of elbow there, too, Barney? – and Micky Baker. It almost made you glad to be a keeper, seeing bits of agg like that. But the funny thing was, by the end of the match everyone would be shaking hands and looking forward to next year's game; being generous in defeat and modest in victory.

Was that what Melvyn Prosser had been doing, a year or so ago in the Athletic boardroom, when he had smiled, and checked that Duffy had enough Slimline, and introduced him to his 'business partner' Charlie Magrudo? And if so, which was Prosser being – generous or modest? Was he admitting Duffy had outsmarted him over the Brendan business, or was he, by introducing Magrudo like that, saying, Nice try, you little short fat goalie, but

I laid out this game so that whatever happened, I won. Was that it? He tried to remember what Prosser had said to him in the Corniche. Something about throwing a lot of bread on the water and most of it getting soggy and being eaten by seagulls. And then something else, about the important thing in business being to look as if you knew what you were doing, even if you didn't. Was that how Melvyn was deliberately behaving for Duffy's benefit?

He must have been right, mustn't he? It must have been Prosser trying to fuck up the club? Nothing else made sense. The planning permission, the connection between Prosser and Magrudo which they'd both tried to deny, the appointment of Jimmy Lister (that *had* been a clever move, he had to hand it to Melvyn), the use of Maggie Coleman to fix both Danny and Brendan, the Layton Road lawsuit. Yes, this had been the final bit of confirmation, when Mr Bullivant had winked and told him he'd sold his house a couple of months before. Sold it before the case came to court, in fact. Well, he wouldn't have bothered, would he?

Proof? That's what they always said, wasn't it – where's your proof? Well, there was proving and knowing, which were two different things in the eyes of the law, but the same thing in the eyes of people who weren't in the court-room. For instance, take the spectators at this Reliables game: that middle-aged man and his wife, both swaddled in toning sheepskin jackets of a mid-brown colour. If they had watched the first half attentively, and then the first ten minutes of the second half, they would know, wouldn't they, that the pub team had decided at half-time to sit on Ken Marriott, and that the Reliables had decided to sit on the speedy little ginge? They wouldn't be able to *prove* it, and they wouldn't understand about Geoff Bell's technology, but they would see it and know it. And they'd be right, too, wouldn't they?

Uh-huh. The first ten minutes were over, with both the ginge and Maggot slightly the worse for wear. Now came the tricky bit. Two extra men pushing forward, looking for the killer goal. No time for mistakes, no time for Maggot's vision. Still, the Reliables had swapped their full-backs over, and that seemed to be making a difference: not too much coming down the flanks at the moment. They seemed to be shooting from a bit further out, too. Like that – whoops, thought Duffy, as the big pub centre-back who'd been pushing up tanked the ball from thirty yards out. He started moving right and down, but suddenly the ball wasn't coming. It had struck Geoff Bell on the hip and squirted sideways to Maggot. Duffy, from where he lay on the ground, watched Maggot look up, pick out Karl French up front, measure his pass, and hit it quickly.

What had young French said? 'Great vision. Great vision. Only trouble is, the ball doesn't go *anywhere fucking near* where he wants it to.' Maggot's pass went quickly off course, but as Duffy got to his feet again, he saw that the ball had unerringly picked out Barney, the Reliables' other front man – the one characterised as fat and smarmy, according to Geoff's earpiece. Barney gave a fat sideways glance and smarmily transferred the ball to French. Christ, he *was* fast, thought Duffy, as young Karl set off. Took three yards out of his marker in the first ten. Thirty yards out, only the fullback and the keeper ahead of him. Getting pushed too wide by the full-back – no, that was just a bluff, and suddenly French had cut back into the middle and skinned the back in the process. Closing on the keeper – Duffy didn't know who to root for. On this occasion professional solidarity lost out. Do it, Karl, Duffy found himself urging. Do the biz. He almost couldn't look. Karl did the biz – drew the keeper, waited for him to go down, slid the ball under his diving body. One–one. 'GOAL,' roared Duffy from his unpopulated end of the pitch, 'GOOOAAAL.' Karl French had turned away from the prostrate pub keeper, and stood with both forearms raised in triumph. His team-mates descended and embraced him. I suppose that's what they call French kissing, thought Duffy. Perhaps one or two of the team ought to take French lessons.

Ha. Maggie Coleman. That was where he'd blown it. Of course, she was one tough tart, but he should have known that, shouldn't he? You can't put the arm on tarts that easily. Still eager to play the copper after all these years, Duffy. Sure, he'd had excuses – the real coppers would have closed down Maggie once Jimmy Lister had given them Geoff Bell's photos – and he'd wanted to clear up his bit of bother before they did theirs. What he'd done, he now saw, was to screw both sides. She wouldn't tell him who was paying her; and then, before the real coppers could get to her, she'd disappeared. Done a runner; packed up a few things from her flat off Twyford Avenue and scarpered. Never seen again. Moved up east, perhaps, changed her name – who knows? It meant, of course, that the charges against Brendan were officially dropped, but there would have been more satisfactory ways of doing that in the first place. Like by getting Maggie sent down for conspiring to pervert the course of justice and seeing Melvyn Prosser go down with her.

The breeze was freshening behind Duffy. The corner flags to left and right of him were pointing straight up the touchline. Well, that should wear down the pub side a bit. No one likes facing a stiff wind in the second half if they haven't had the benefit of it in the first: some elementary sense of justice makes you feel affronted. Still, that didn't seem too ... oh shit, the ginge, oh, ooooh, aah, *now* ... a thump on his wrist as Duffy dived to his left and the ball pinged away for a corner.

'Save, keeper.'

'Great stuff, Duff.'

Duffy bounced about on his goal line while the tallest pub defender stood directly in front of him and tried to block his view of the corner. It was an outswinger – he could tell that from the start. He came for it, the wind got hold of the ball, and Duffy was being dragged far out of goal. The all-or-nothing ball the keeper hates: the point at which you're either a hero or a wally. There's nothing in between. Not a wally, Duffy thought, *not a wally*, as he snatched the ball from the path of an approaching pubman. Four steps and he was at the edge of his area. A memory of Athletic's last game of the previous season flashed at him. With the breeze behind, he hoofed a drop kick at the ball. Oh shit. Well, sometimes a wally, he reflected: the ball skidded slightly as he struck it, and flew directly into touch on the halfway line. Sometimes a wally, Duffy, sometimes. But I do have this vision, you see.

Mel Prosser had vision – vision of a fortune. Charlie Magrudo had vision of a parkful of bulldozers and changing his filthy Granada more often. Jimmy Lister had vision of Athletic playing cultured one-touch stuff in the lower reaches of the Third Division. Brendan Domingo had vision of not being booed every time he touched the ball. Mr Joyce had vision of a country where Brendan Domingo had no place at all.

What about Mr Joyce and the Red White and Blue? That was the one bit Duffy was prepared to put down to coincidence. An awkward coincidence, but it might well have been one: on the whole, he thought Prosser a bit too clever, and a bit too careful, to get tangled up with psychos like Mr Joyce. Unless – was he that clever? Duffy had once been picked up by a chubby journalist at the Alligator who had told him, 'Never overestimate your opponent.' He'd thought it just a smart line at the time, but it had some truth. Prosser, after all, had said that the thing about business was looking as if you knew what you were doing. And Prosser, when it came down to it, hadn't succeeded in his main ambition: fucking up the club he owned. You'd think, wouldn't you, that anyone would be able to do that? Maybe he wasn't so clever?

At the start of the present season Melvyn Prosser had made a great noise about having every confidence in Jimmy Lister. Perhaps he meant that he had every confidence in Jimmy Lister's ability to get Athletic relegated second time round. So Jimmy started the season as boss, and a slightly different boss from the previous year. He was even quoted in the *Chronicle* as saying, 'I don't want any fanny merchants in my squad. Hard work is what wins matches.' No cultured England B wing-halves for Jimmy Lister.

Halfway through the season hard work had helped Athletic into a decent mid-table position, Jimmy had bought himself six new pairs of white shoes, and Melvyn Prosser had sold out. Just as there are always new players coming through, there are always new businessmen coming through, and Melvyn Prosser found Ricky De Souza, a bright lad with a chain of grocer's shops and a sense that owning a football club was about the most

English thing you could do. Ricky De Souza reached an understanding with the Reform Group, which quite frankly had been pissing Melvyn off with all the agg they'd been giving him, and the deal was struck.

The sick joke of it all was that as soon as Melvyn handed the club over to Ricky, Athletic began to slide. One or two injuries, a run of tough away games to top clubs, two–one defeats that could as well have been two–one victories, and suddenly the club was in the bottom six. And this time round, Jimmy Lister didn't have Brendan Domingo to pull the side together. Brendan's little floorshow had won him what he'd hoped: release from the terms of his contract. Brendan was now snuggling down with a nice mid-table Second Division outfit up north, where they had two other black players in the first-team squad, and where the local yobbos appreciated his silky skills. 'Silky Domingo' they'd taken to calling him, with something close to affection.

So this time round, it might be serious for Athletic and Ricky De Souza. Duffy would watch the results of their last ten games this season with more than a little interest. But if they carried on at their present rate, by this time next year Athletic would be in the Fourth Division, Jimmy Lister would be on a slow camel to Abu Dhabi, Ricky De Souza would be thinking he'd bought a real dog of a club, and Melvyn Prosser would be kicking himself very hard indeed.

Odd how there was always some consolation. Most of the time you didn't win five–nil, and you didn't lose five–nil. Often things ended in a sort of draw. Duffy's match with Melvyn Prosser had ended in a sort of draw. One–one, you could say. You could say it with even more certainty about the present game: Reliables versus

Pubmen. Technically, there were still a few minutes to go, but the ref was running short of wind and wouldn't mind at all getting home early for his dinner, so he blew and waved his arm in a big circle over his head like the refs did on TV, and the players trooped off, and Ken Marriott shook hands with the speedy little ginge, and the pubmen thought, well it's not a bad fixture, this, what with the half-bottle of whisky, and they don't push us *that* hard do they, still, pity about that soft goal we gave away, real sucker punch. Duffy thought, if it hadn't been for that ginge I'd have kept a clean sheet.

'Nice work, Geoff,' he said as he walked off with Bell.

'Yeah, thanks, I really upped my workrate in the second half.' Duffy had actually been referring to the nice work Geoff had done at half-time, but didn't like to withdraw the compliment now.

'Did they really say that thing about me being a bit small for a keeper?'

Bell nodded.

'Afraid so, Duffy. Sorry about that. The only thing I made up was the bit about Karl French.'

'What, about him being out of his depth in this class of game?'

'Yeah, that bit. Well, I thought it might gee him up. He hadn't done much, first half, had he?'

'You clever old thing.' Duffy was genuinely admiring.

'Well, I'm not just a pretty face.'

They clattered up the two stone steps to the changing hut, into an atmosphere of steam, and shouting, and snapping wet towels, and fake screeches, and first cigarettes, and the odd hip-flask, and bare, scrubbed bums which didn't give Duffy a momentary twitch. Odd that, he thought, because I must be in the clear now: I won't end up tinkling my leper's bell on some Welsh mountain-side. He checked his armpits, looked down at his legs in a ritual way, but he felt, after all this time, that he was almost certainly in the clear. Maybe it took some time before you got your confidence back, he thought. It can't be that I don't fancy guys any more. Things don't change that quickly. I hope they don't, anyway.

Things did change that quickly for some. As he sat on the hard, slatted bench waiting his turn in the shower, Duffy remembered a long, pale face and a curly black perm that was beginning to grow out. Danny Matson. A dozen first-team games, a sniff of the big time, free entry to The Knight Spot, striking up an understanding with big Brendan, photo in the papers, popular with the girls, waiting delivery on the new Capri, and then ... *phut*. You're a small feature in somebody else's plans and your career goes down the toilet. Never knowing why, never knowing who. Left with a few thoughts about football being a cruel game and a folded picture of Trevor Brooking's room. Where was Danny Matson now?

If you enjoyed

Putting the Boot In

why not try the other novels in
Dan Kavanagh's gripping crime series

*Available now and
coming soon from Orion*